Camp Club Girls

McKenzie's
OREGON
OPERATION

© 2010 by Barbour Publishing, Inc.

Edited by Jeanette Littleton.

ISBN 978-1-60260-294-6

Cover design: Thinkpen Design

Published by Barbour Publishing, Inc., P.O. Box 719, Uhrichsville, Ohio 44683, www.barbourbooks.com

Our mission is to publish and distribute inspirational products offering exceptional value and biblical encouragement to the masses.

ecpa Member of the
Evangelical Christian
Publishers Association

Printed in the United States of America.
Dickinson Press, Inc.; Grand Rapids, MI; October 2010; D10002531

Camp Club Girls

McKenzie's OREGON OPERATION

Shari Barr

BARBOUR
PUBLISHING

CHAPTER 1

Lost!

"They're going to hit us!" McKenzie screamed, clutching the sides of the tiny sailboat, *Sea Skimmer*.

Alexis Howell reached back and grabbed the tiller, the steering device of the boat. She tried to move the sailboat out of the path of the motorboat speeding straight for them. But the steady breeze from earlier had died down.

Instead of moving out of the motorboat's way, the *Sea Skimmer* bobbed lazily, its sails hanging limp. Alex paddled frantically with her hands, but her attempts were useless.

"Watch out!" McKenzie cried. She waved one arm furiously, trying to get the driver's attention.

A man wearing a black baseball cap and mirrored sunglasses sat in the driver's seat. He stared straight ahead as if unaware of the girls. The woman in the front seat beside him looked the other way as they barreled down on the skimmer.

McKenzie and Alex yelled, but the roar of the motorboat drowned their screams.

Zoom! Splash! Suddenly the driver whipped the boat into a sharp turn.

But that caused choppy waves rolling right at the girls. Again and again. Higher and higher. They relentlessly beat the sailboat.

"Hold on!" Alex cried out.

The skimmer bobbed wildly.

Blam! Whoosh!

The sailboat toppled, dumping the girls into the blue-green ocean water.

Ahh! With flailing arms, McKenzie began to sink. Seconds later she felt an upward pull. Her orange life vest popped her out of the water. She bounced up and down as the waves slowed. She coughed and sputtered from the salty water that had gone up her nose. Craning her neck, she searched for Alexis.

"Alex!" McKenzie yelled, her eyes skimming the surface of the water. "Where are you?"

The capsized sailboat lifted slightly. Alex's sunburned face appeared. "I'm under here. You okay?"

"Great," McKenzie said between sputters. "Except for a major wedgie."

"Wow, what was that all about?" Alex asked. She slipped from beneath the overturned skimmer, clinging to its side.

McKenzie flung her wet hair out of her eyes. She swam to the sailboat. Then she draped her arms across the bottom until she caught her breath. "Man, was that guy trying to kill us or what? I thought for sure we were goners!"

"I don't think he even saw us until he almost hit us," Alexis said. She took a deep breath.

"How could he not see us?" McKenzie asked. "It's hard to miss this skimmer with its bright sails. And he didn't even stop to see if we were okay."

McKenzie squinted into the distance. The motorboat was idling about a half mile away. The driver appeared to be standing and watching them through binoculars. Was he checking to make sure they were okay? If so, why didn't he just come back and ask? She scanned the cove, but only saw a cloud of haze on the horizon.

"Let's swim this thing to shore," Alex suggested. "We'll never be able to turn it right side up out here."

The girls had entered a narrow inlet near Sea Lion Harbor on the Oregon coast. The nearest shoreline was an isolated beach about one hundred yards away. Kicking their legs, the girls slowly towed the sailboat to shore.

A few minutes later, McKenzie felt sand beneath her feet and stood in chest-high water. The girls flipped the sailboat right side up. Then they tugged it onto the sandy beach, far from the incoming tide.

McKenzie flopped onto the sand. Glancing around, she noticed nothing but a small sandy beach along the rocky coastline. "I wonder where we are," she said, slipping out of her life vest. She flung it to the ground.

"I think we're near your Aunt Becca's beach house," Alex said, brushing sand from between her toes. "I try to pay attention to landmarks. Dad taught me to always watch my surroundings. I haven't got lost yet. If we get out of this inlet, we'll be able to see the house just south a little ways, I'm sure."

"I'm glad you know how to sail." McKenzie wrung water out of her dripping curly auburn hair.

"My grandparents' home in San Francisco is on the beach, so my parents take my brothers and me sailing about once a month," Alex said, tucking her dark, shoulder-length curls behind her ears. "I didn't realize the ocean is so much rougher up here, though. No wonder we don't see any more sailboats out here. The water's colder, too."

"I have no clue where we are. I was just looking for the sea lions."

"Aren't sea lions cool? I've seen tons of them near my grandparents' home," Alex said.

McKenzie picked up a seashell and examined it.

"Are they Steller sea lions?" she asked, glancing at her younger friend.

"Yes. Most of the sea lions along the Pacific coast are from the Steller family."

"Why are these kind called Steller?" McKenzie asked.

"They're named after the guy who first studied the animals back in the 1700s," Alex explained. "They're usually larger and lighter in color than other sea lions, the California sea lions. Sea lions are my favorite animal, and sea lion pups are so cute. I can't wait to find those two you were talking about—Mario and Bianca."

"Yeah, it's really weird," McKenzie said. "They're always with their mom, Susie. I saw them last night after my plane got in, before you arrived. But no one's seen them since. I want to put them in my video report."

"I can't believe this report is really going to be on TV. Can you?" Alex asked, shielding her eyes against the sun.

"Not really," McKenzie said. "I about freaked out when the public TV guy called and told me that I had won the essay contest about endangered animals. I couldn't believe it when he said I'd also won a trip to Sea Lion Harbor to film my report."

Alex smiled at her friend. "I am so glad you asked me to come up here and run the video camera. We'll have a blast."

"Mom and Dad would never have agreed to let me come if Aunt Becca wasn't already working out here at the resort. They're too busy on the farm to take a vacation right now, so this is perfect. And it would have been no fun to spend every day alone while Becca's at work," McKenzie said, digging a broken seashell from the sand and tossing it aside. "Though it's cool to have an aunt who's a private airplane pilot with a company connected to a resort!"

She stood, hopping across the sand until the waves washed over her toes. This was her first visit to the ocean, and she absolutely loved it. The Oregon coast was a long way from her parents' farm in Montana. The salty air mixed with the scent of pine trees was so different from the woodsy smells back home.

Last night, after Aunt Becca had picked McKenzie up at the airport, she had taken her to a spot farther down the coast so McKenzie could see the Pacific Ocean. The roar of the waves had practically hypnotized her. She had never heard or seen anything like it. The water here at Sea Lion Harbor, though, was calm compared to the way the ocean had been the night before.

"Let's go exploring," Alex said, interrupting McKenzie's thoughts.

Alex had already started down the short stretch

of sandy beach that lay between two craggy rock formations. McKenzie followed her, wet sand squishing between her toes. Alex hurried to the nearest rock and scurried to the top.

"Come on up." Alex motioned for McKenzie to follow. "You've got to see this."

The rocks were rough and hot beneath McKenzie's feet, but she scaled the rock to stand beside Alex. Below the girls lay a narrow sandy inlet that stretched into a gaping hole in the side of the cliff.

"Wow!" McKenzie exclaimed. "Look at this cave."

McKenzie climbed partway down the rock before leaping the last few feet. She fell to her knees, reaching her arms out to keep from falling on her face. She stood and brushed the sand off her legs. The sandbar was cool here, shaded by the craggy rocks towering above the opening to the cave.

McKenzie turned as Alex leaped off the rock beside her. The girls moved closer together. They stared into the opening of the cave that yawned like a huge mouth.

Alex's blue eyes gleamed with wonder. "Look how tall it is. You could drive a truck through there. That is, if you could get a truck out here."

McKenzie took a few steps forward. She approached the opening and felt the cool, damp air inside. She wrinkled her nose. "Pew! It smells like something died in there."

"Are you going in?" Alex sniffed the air with a look of disgust.

"I'm a wimp. You go first." McKenzie gave Alex a gentle shove forward.

"Why me?" Alex said, taking a step backward. "You're a whole year older than I am."

McKenzie sighed as she shook her head. "Okay, okay. But you're coming with me," she said, tugging her friend's arm.

McKenzie stepped inside the cave, letting her eyes adjust to the darkness. Nothing but a black hole loomed before her. She had no idea how far the tunnel reached into the cliff. She glanced downward and noticed a paper fast-food cup lying on the sand at her feet.

"Hey, look. Somebody's been here." McKenzie pointed at the cup.

"Maybe it's been here awhile," Alex said as she bent over and picked it up.

"I don't think so," McKenzie answered. "The cup hasn't even started to get soggy. I think someone was here not too long ago. Or maybe somebody is still here."

McKenzie shuddered as she spoke the words. Standing in the cave without a light was starting to give her the willies. She turned to make sure Alex had followed her. *I'm thinking this isn't exactly the place*

I want to explore without a guide. On the other hand, maybe I don't want to explore it at all.

"Maybe this isn't such a good idea," Alex said. "We can't see where we're going without a flashlight."

"I agree. I'm not about to get lost in this place. It's way too creepy for me. Besides, my feet are cold," McKenzie said, rubbing the goose bumps forming on her arms. Her wet swimsuit felt icy against her skin. Eager for the warmth of the sun outside, she hurried toward the entrance. After stepping from the darkness of the cave, she stopped in her tracks.

A thick blanket of fog was creeping across the smooth surface of the cove toward them. The sun that had warmed them earlier had disappeared behind the haze.

"We'd better go before the fog closes in on us." Alex sprinted toward the rock piling and quickly climbed to the top. "I want to be able to see our way back."

Dashing back to the beach, they hurried into their life jackets. Then they carried the *Sea Skimmer* to the cold water's edge.

"Hop on," Alex said as she steadied the boat. "I'll tow us out into deeper water."

McKenzie pulled herself up, the boat teetering as she climbed aboard. Alex waded out a little farther, pulling the boat behind her. A few seconds later she pulled herself onto the deck of the boat, tipping the skimmer slightly. McKenzie gripped the sides praying Alex wouldn't tip the boat over.

"I'll teach you to sail sometime," Alex said, grabbing a stick that was fastened to the floor of the sailboat. "But not today."

McKenzie watched in amazement as Alex's hands flew back and forth. "What is that thingy?" she asked, pointing to a sticklike device attached to the floor.

"It's called a tiller. It's connected to the rudder, so I can steer the boat. It will even let us sail against the wind," Alex answered. "But barely any breeze is blowing now. We're not going anywhere very fast."

Alex turned the tiller, trying to catch what little breeze they could in the orange, yellow, and blue sail. *Turtles can swim faster than this*, McKenzie thought as Alex steered the skimmer into deeper water.

Minutes later they sailed out of the inlet into the open waters of the cove. McKenzie focused on the fog pressing closer and closer. The water shimmered like an aquamarine stone, an occasional breeze causing slight ripples on the surface. Alex caught every puff of wind, no matter how small, and slowly sailed the boat toward home.

McKenzie had never sailed before. She had only ridden in speedboats and rowboats on lakes near her home in Montana. She gazed toward the shore, noting the unfamiliar landmarks. Nothing but pine trees and steep bluffs lined the shoreline.

"Are you sure you know where we are? None of this looks familiar to me. Shouldn't there be houses along the beach?" McKenzie's grip on the side of the boat tightened.

Alex kept her hand on the tiller and gazed at the overcast sky. She looked up and down the mainland. Then she brought her free hand up and chewed on a fingernail.

Alex's eyes looked worried. "I thought I paid a lot of attention earlier, but I don't recognize anything. Those trees aren't familiar, and I don't see the resort. I'm not sure where we are. I guess maybe I was watching for sea lions more than I thought."

McKenzie felt her stomach lurch. "What do you mean? We aren't lost, are we?"

Alex fixed her gaze on the mainland, struggling to keep the sailboat from going too far into the open cove. "I'll figure it out in a minute," she finally said.

Uh-oh, McKenzie thought as she stared at the isolated shoreline. *I sure hope she figures it out, because I have no clue where we are.*

"Alex, I just had an awful thought," McKenzie stammered. "Aunt Becca was already at work when we left. I forgot to tell anyone we were leaving."

15

Alex blinked her eyes nervously. "We were supposed to tell Mr. Carney if we went sailing, weren't we?"

Mr. Carney, or Mr. C. as the girls called him, rented the cabin next door to Aunt Becca. He was an elderly man who, he said, had rented the same cabin every summer for the last twenty years. Since Aunt Becca had rented the same cabin for the previous three years, the two knew each other well. Mr. Carney had volunteered to keep an eye on the girls if they needed anything while Becca was at work.

"Nobody knows where we are," McKenzie said, her voice trembling. "Aunt Becca won't know we're missing until she gets home from work. That won't be for hours yet."

"Mr. C. will notice that our sailboat is missing," Alex said, trying to sound reassuring.

"What if he's not home?" McKenzie asked, growing more worried by the minute.

Alex didn't answer. The girls sat in silence, watching the fog roll toward them. It settled over them like a cold vapor. McKenzie could barely see past Alex on the other end of the boat.

The sails of the little sailboat hung limply as the breeze died. The *Sea Skimmer* bobbed idly. McKenzie shut her eyes briefly, feeling the gentle rise and fall of the boat. *Dear God,* she prayed. *Keep us safe and help us find our way home.*

"Have you figured it out yet?" McKenzie asked as she cautiously opened her eyes.

Alex turned to McKenzie, her voice faltering. "I. . . I. . .can hardly see anything through the fog. I don't know where the homes and the docks and the resort are. Oh, McKenzie, I think we're lost!"

Kidnapped!

A shiver ran down McKenzie's spine. "Shouldn't we just try to reach shore?" she asked, her voice higher than normal.

"The shoreline here is mostly rocks," Alex pointed out. "So there could be lots of underwater rocks to get caught up on. We don't want to get too close until I know just where we are."

The little sailboat floated listlessly. Only a few minutes earlier the sky had been clear. Now dense fog had settled over the cove, surrounding them in a white, swirling mist.

"What are we going to do?" McKenzie asked fearfully.

Alex chewed her bottom lip as she surveyed the situation. "Look!" she exclaimed, pointing at a flash of light cutting through the fog. "There's the light from the Heceta Head Lighthouse up the coast. We have to head back to our left to make sure we stay in the cove. I sure don't want to get out in the open waters."

McKenzie wasn't used to the ocean. The thought of being swept out into the rough waters scared her. "You don't think. . .we'll get washed away. . . ." Her voice cut off.

"Oh, of course not," Alex said with a smile.

A fake smile, McKenzie thought. *She's trying not to scare me. She doesn't want me to know we're in big, big trouble.* McKenzie's hand clutched the sides of the sailboat until her knuckles turned white.

"We can't even see where we are." McKenzie's voice trembled. "How will we know if we're being pulled out to sea?"

"The tide's coming in. It'll push us into the shore, not away from it," Alex reassured her.

"It'll push us into the rocks, you mean?" McKenzie shivered. *Why, oh why, didn't we tell Mr. C. we were going sailing?*

"I think we're just in a little pocket of fog. The sun is trying to break through," Alex said as she turned the sails, trying to catch what little breeze she could.

A seagull cried overhead, and a motorboat puttered in the distance.

At least someone else is out here. If we could only see, McKenzie thought, *then we could ask for help.*

"I'm really sorry I didn't pay more attention. I'm the one who got us lost," Alex said softly.

McKenzie smiled slightly. "It's not any more your

fault than it is mine. I shouldn't have been gawking around so much. Anyway, I can't believe God would let us get lost at sea. I've been praying."

"Yeah, I have, too." Alex sighed. "I guess we have to trust Him."

McKenzie nodded. Though she still couldn't see the shoreline, she felt more relaxed than she had earlier. As she peered into the fog, a sleek gray object slid through the water beside her. She jumped. A whiskered nose popped through the water. For a second, McKenzie couldn't speak, then she cried, "Susie! Boy, am I glad to see you."

The sea lion spun in the water, twirling like a ballerina. Her flippers flapped up and down as she performed her water dance.

"Alex," McKenzie turned to her friend, "this is the sea lion I was telling you about."

"You mean her pups are the ones that are missing?" Alex asked, working the tiller.

"Yes," McKenzie said, relieved. "We can't be too far from Sea Lion Harbor."

Aaarrr! Aaarrr! Susie barked as she splashed the water with her flippers. With a final spin, the sea lion slipped away from the boat.

"I think she's calling for her pups," Alex said. "I hope she finds them."

A cool breeze brushed McKenzie's face. The bright sails snapped as they caught the breeze that suddenly rolled in across the cove.

"Hey, we're moving now." Alex grinned at McKenzie.

"Look." McKenzie pointed at Susie, barely visible in the fog. "Maybe we should follow her."

Alex steered in Susie's direction. The sea lion swam slowly, as if waiting for the sailboat to keep up.

"I think the fog is lifting. I see some trees on the shore." Alex brushed her damp hair out of her eyes.

McKenzie relaxed her grip on the sailboat and breathed deeply. She saw the vague outline of one the resort's beach homes. "God must have heard us. He sent good ol' Susie to show us the way back."

Minutes later Susie had disappeared, but the girls had sailed out of the cloud of fog. Alex steered the boat toward Becca's boat dock, clearly visible in the emerging sunlight. After Alex hopped onto the dock, she tied up the boat.

McKenzie's knees wobbled as she tried to stand. She flailed her arms back and forth like a windmill as the skimmer teetered from side to side.

"Here, grab my hand!" Alex cried.

McKenzie grabbed Alex's fingertips and leaped onto the dock. "I've never been so glad to touch dry land before."

"I told you we'd get back okay," Alex said as she started up the dock. "I've never lost anyone yet."

McKenzie shook her head teasingly. "Okay, I'll never not trust you again."

As the girls approached their beach house, a voice called. Turning to the neighboring house, McKenzie saw Mr. Carney sitting in the shade in his lawn chair. A glass of iced tea sat in a wire cup holder beside him. The white stubble on his balding head contrasted with his black skin.

"Hi, Mr. C.," McKenzie called out, jogging over to him. "This is my friend Alexis Howell, but everybody calls her Alex. She came from Sacramento to spend the week with me."

Mr. Carney stood and shook Alex's hand, his teeth flashing a wide smile. "Nice to meet you, Miss Alex. You're quite the sailor."

"Thank you, I've had quite a bit of practice. Except I don't like sailing in the fog."

"You girls had me worried. I was about ready to call the Coast Guard. But then I saw your little skimmer. That fog can be tricky." Mr. Carney scratched his head with his pinkie finger. "And girls, this ocean is too rough to take a sailboat out of the protected bay and into the ocean."

"Lucky for us, we saw Susie and she led us back

home." McKenzie unzipped her life jacket and slid it off.

"That wasn't luck, young lady." Mr. Carney's eyes grew serious. "The good Lord was looking after you two, He was. If I hadn't seen you leave, no one would have known where you went. You could have been in a heap of trouble out there if the fog hadn't lifted when it did."

McKenzie glanced sheepishly toward Alex and met her gaze. She knew Mr. Carney was speaking the truth. They could have been in serious trouble.

"I'm not scolding you girls, but I know your Aunt Becca had already left for work when you set out. She asked me to keep an eye out for you while she's gone. You just had me a bit worried, that's all."

"We're sorry we worried you. We were hoping to find Susie's pups. I want to show them to Alex," McKenzie explained. "Has anybody seen them yet this morning?"

Mr. Carney shook his head as he settled back in his lawn chair. "Not that I know of. It's strange, if you ask me. Those little pups are always with their momma. Don't know what could have happened to them."

"Do you think a whale or a shark could have gotten them?" Alexis shuddered.

Mr. Carney shrugged his shoulders. "I suppose that's possible, but I really don't think it's likely. Susie keeps a close watch over her pups."

The elderly man glanced at his watch and rose to his feet. "I'd better go check my lunch in the oven, then I'm heading to the gift shop. The book I ordered about caves came in this morning."

"We were going over there to shop for souvenirs," McKenzie said. "We could pick it up for you if you want."

Mr. Carney accepted the offer and pulled his wallet from his back pocket. After he handed them a couple of bills, they ran across the sand to Aunt Becca's rental house. McKenzie found the key her aunt kept hidden on the front porch, and they slipped inside the back door.

Aunt Becca's golden retriever met them at the door. "Hey there, Mickey." McKenzie scratched the dog's head as she headed toward the computer in the corner of the living room.

"I'm going to check my e-mail before we go." McKenzie clicked the mouse until her account popped up.

"Hey, you've got a message from Inspector Gadget." Alex giggled as she peered over her shoulder and saw their friend Kate's name on the screen. "Oh, and there's another one from Elizabeth. But there's nothing from any of the other Camp Club Girls, though."

The Camp Club Girls were McKenzie's roommates from camp in Arizona. The six girls came from all parts of the country and had become best friends.

While at camp they had solved a mystery together. Now when the girls visited each other, they always managed to solve some sort of mystery or riddle. They called their friend Kate Oliver Inspector Gadget because she had every new gadget or electronic device imaginable. Kate was eleven years old and lived in Philadelphia.

"I e-mailed all the girls as soon as I found out about the missing sea lion pups. Maybe Kate has some advice."

Kate had written:

Hey roomies, anything new about the pups? Dad gave me a pair of video sunglasses that are really cool. You can record sights and sounds when you're wearing them and nobody will know. I'm sending them to you so you should have them in a couple of days. They might come in handy to solve this mystery.

"Cool!" Alex said, peering over her shoulder. "I can't wait to see those."

"I didn't even know they made video sunglasses," McKenzie said, clicking on a message from fourteen-year-old Elizabeth Anderson, who lived in Amarillo, Texas.

Hi McKenzie and Alex,
Ever since you told me about the sea lion pups,
I've been praying and praying. I have the strangest
feeling that the pups are still alive. I think God
wants you to save them, just like He does us. Keep
all us Camp Club Girls posted so we can help.
Love, Elizabeth

McKenzie logged off, feeling relieved after reading Elizabeth's words. The older girl had an amazing faith. McKenzie often wished she was more like her. Elizabeth always remembered to turn to God, while McKenzie often forgot.

The girls changed quickly out of their swimsuits into shorts and T-shirts. Ten minutes later, they walked through the front door of the lobby to Emerald Bay Resort and Cottages.

Two employees stood behind a counter, busy with customers making reservations on computers. A rock fireplace stood at one end of the lobby with a leather couch and chairs nestled around it. A display of vacation brochures sat on the polished wooden coffee table in front.

A pamphlet caught McKenzie's eye as she approached the table. "Hey, look at this, Alex." She grabbed a colorful brochure and skimmed the front page. "Newport, a city just north of here, is having a photography contest during their festival later this week. Why don't you enter? You're a great photographer."

Alex took the brochure from McKenzie, her blue eyes sparkling. "Ooh. This would be fun. Maybe I could take pictures of some of the whales."

McKenzie grabbed a handful of various brochures and flicked through them. "We could go to the Heceta Head Lighthouse and Cape Perpetua. You should be able to get some really good shots up there."

The girls settled onto the couch with their heads together, poring over the brochures. McKenzie looked up when she heard loud voices at the counter.

"We reserved the Hideaway Bungalow more than three months ago." A dark-haired man with sunglasses perched on his head snapped at a young man behind the counter. A woman with blond hair stood beside him, shaking her head with exasperation.

They look familiar, McKenzie thought. *Where have I seen them?*

"I'm sorry, Mr. Franks," the clerk apologized. "Apparently there has been some confusion. We just gave that cabin to another party. But I'll tell you what I'll do. You can have the Beachside Cabin at the same rate as the Hideaway. That's quite an upgrade. The Beachside has a magnificent view of the cove."

Mr. Franks slapped his hand on the counter. "I don't want the Beachside Cabin. I reserved the Hideaway, and I demand that I get it!"

"Uhh," the clerk stammered as his face turned red. "But that's not possible."

"Young man," the bleach-blond woman said in a syrupy sweet voice. "I'm sure you don't understand our predicament. We're trainers at Sea Park, and we always reserve the Hideaway since it's away from all the hustle and bustle of the resort. It's an understanding we have with your manager, Mr. Simms. I'm sure you can make the necessary arrangements immediately, can't you?"

"Oh. . .uh," the clerk stuttered as he pecked on his computer keyboard. "I am so sorry. I didn't realize you were *the* Mel and Tia Franks. Let me double-check. Aah, yes, the Hideaway has just been cleaned, as a matter of fact. I can give you your keys now."

McKenzie raised her eyebrows as she met Alex's gaze. She tried to suppress a giggle as the irate couple grabbed their keys and marched out of the lobby.

"Now I know where I've seen them," McKenzie whispered to Alex. "Aren't they the couple in the motorboat that almost ran over us?"

"Yeah, I think you're right," Alex said, watching the couple through the window.

After shoving the free brochures in her back

pocket, McKenzie headed across the lobby to the gift shop. Alex stopped to look at a postcard display, but McKenzie headed to an aisle filled with trinkets. She picked up a gray stuffed sea lion. It barked when she pressed its stomach.

Evan would like this, she thought, trying to decide what to get her little brother for a souvenir. *Or maybe he'd like the glow-in-the-dark Ping-Pong balls or a monster-sized stuffed whale.*

A rack held various hats with fake hair attached to the underside. An army green fishing hat had stringy red hair hanging down. Black bushy hair stuck out from beneath an orange stocking cap. She picked up a baseball cap that had two long blond braids attached. Twisting her hair into a knot, she tucked it under the cap as she shoved it onto her head.

"Can I help you, ma'am?" McKenzie asked with a forced Southern drawl as she approached her friend in the next aisle.

Alex looked up from the postcard in her hand. Her blue eyes sparkled as she burst out laughing. "Where did you get that? You should see yourself."

McKenzie led Alex to the goofy hat display. The girls each grabbed a cap and giggled as they modeled for each other.

After they had tried on nearly every style,

McKenzie decided to get a green fishing hat for Evan and a T-shirt for herself. Alex had a handful of postcards and a bag of gum balls. While the girls paid for their souvenirs, they inquired about Mr. Carney's book. The clerk located it beneath the checkout counter and handed it to them. After paying for it, the girls stepped outside.

"This looks like a cool book." McKenzie scanned the cover and read aloud, *"Secluded Caves along the Oregon Coast: Little-known Caves for Amateur Spelunkers."*

"What are spelunkers?" Alex asked, popping a gum ball in her mouth.

"Cave explorers." McKenzie flipped through the book as she walked across the parking lot, pausing to look at some of the pictures. "Maybe I can borrow this from Mr. C. when he's done."

McKenzie closed the book and stuck it back in the bag with her other purchases. The girls walked down the winding lane to Mr. Carney's cottage. After they delivered the book, he promised she could borrow it when he was finished.

Since Aunt Becca wouldn't get home from work for several more hours, the girls decided to have a picnic on the beach. They found a spot they liked in the bright sun and settled on the sand.

A woman stretched out on a lounge chair beneath a huge yellow beach umbrella. A girl who looked about six years old and a boy of about nine were building a sand castle near the water. The girl carried buckets of sand while the boy pounded the sand into shapes. So far, their castle looked like a bunch of lumps.

While the girls ate, the kids' voices drifted up the beach.

"I want to see the sea lion pups," the little girl said as she dumped a pail full of wet sand next to the castle.

"You can't see them," the boy said, patting the sand into a cone shape. "They're gone."

"Where did they go?" the girl asked. She plunked onto the beach and folded her arms across her chest.

"How do I know?" the boy answered, dumping another bucket of sand. "A man and woman took them away this morning."

McKenzie stopped chewing and leaned forward. She held her breath and a tingle ran up her neck as the boy continued. "I saw them. Mario and Bianca were kidnapped!"

CHAPTER 3

An Intriguing Invitation

"Did that kid say what I think he did?" McKenzie asked, nudging Alex.

"Did he say somebody kidnapped Mario and Bianca?" Alex said, with her mouth full of sandwich.

A banana slice fell out of McKenzie's sandwich on its way to her mouth. It rolled down her front, smearing a glob of peanut butter down her swimsuit. "That's what I thought he said, too."

McKenzie plucked the banana off her lap and stuffed it in her mouth. She turned her attention back to the family building the lopsided sand castle.

The mother lifted her head from the lounge chair and turned toward her son. "Did you really see someone take the sea lion pups, Keaton?"

The boy nodded. "I went outside this morning before anyone was up. I saw some guy and a woman pull two little sea lions out of the water and put them into their boat. Two teenagers were helping."

"Did you see what they looked like?" the mom asked as she sprayed sunscreen on the boy's back.

The boy shrugged. He stuck a plastic shovel into the sand, scooping a trench around the castle. "Sort of, but not really. The guy had a really cool giant fish tattoo on his arm. Their boat was silver with red trim."

The mother turned from her son and tossed the sunscreen bottle to the ground. "Claire, get your life jacket on!" she yelled as she chased her daughter, who was running toward the water.

Standing, the boy tossed his shovel to the ground. He grabbed an inner tube and raced down the beach after his mother and sister.

Thank God Mario and Bianca are still alive, McKenzie thought with relief. *Elizabeth was right.* She glanced toward the boats sailing in the cove and sighed. *Five or six boats there now are silver with red trim. How can anyone figure out who took the pups if the boy can't remember what they look like?*

"Do you think someone really stole Mario and Bianca?" Alex took a gulp from her juice bottle.

"That kid seems to think so." McKenzie squirted sunscreen onto her leg and rubbed it in. "But he only remembers the guy's tattoo. Whoever stole them surely wouldn't come back around. They're probably long gone by now."

Alex stuffed her sandwich bags into her tote and nodded. "True. But maybe the kid is just making the whole thing up."

"He sure acted like he knew what he was talking about. I mean, he noticed the guy's tattoo and all. Why would he make that up?"

Alex rubbed sunscreen across her face. "Maybe we could go out there and talk to him. Ask him questions and stuff."

McKenzie looked down the beach and saw the woman gathering towels and sand toys. "I think we're too late."

The mother grabbed the little girl's hand, and the boy tagged along behind, dragging the beach chair. Minutes later they disappeared in the crowd of sunbathers near the resort. The girls ran to the cold water for a few moments, then stretched out on their beach towels.

McKenzie closed her eyes against the sun. Then she remembered she hadn't told the Camp Club Girls about the boy's story of the sea lion pups' kidnapping. She dug her cell phone from her bag and texted a message. She sent it to Kate and Elizabeth, as well as Bailey Chang in Peoria, Illinois, and Sydney Lincoln in Washington DC.

She propped herself up with her elbow and glanced

at Alex. "Why don't we get your camcorder and walk down to Sea Lion Harbor? We might as well get started on the video report."

The girls quickly gathered their towels and bags and headed to the beach house. After changing their clothes, they grabbed their cameras and stepped out the back door. They set off down the road behind the row of beach homes that led to the Sea Lion Harbor observation area.

When they arrived at the overlook, McKenzie heard the sea lions before she saw them. Their barking was unlike anything she had ever heard. Even though she had heard them the night before with Aunt Becca, she was still shocked by the noise.

"Look at them all," McKenzie said, peering over the fence that overlooked the rocky ledge below. "There must be dozens of them. They're so cute when they play, and they're so noisy. Do you know what a group of sea lions is called?"

"A cluster?" Alex asked.

"No, a herd," McKenzie said. "When Aunt Becca told me that, I thought she was kidding. I thought she said it was a herd because I'm used to cows being in herds!"

"Well, I guess they're actually about as big as cows," Alex said.

"At least some of them. I never realized how big

they can get," McKenzie agreed.

"Do you see Susie?" Alex leaned against the railing and watched the sea lions frolic in the water.

McKenzie squinted as she searched the herd for Susie. "There she is! On the ledge. That's not like her. Last night she was spinning like a ballet dancer while Mario and Bianca swam around her. She must not have found her pups yet. She looks sad now."

"Maybe she misses her babies." Alex lifted her camcorder and focused on the sea lions below her.

McKenzie focused her digital camera on Susie and snapped a picture. Several of the sea lions were chasing fish, catching them playfully, then letting them go. "Susie just doesn't act right. Do you think we could figure out what happened to the pups?"

Alex lowered her camcorder. "I think we should try, anyway. When I was doing my report for school, I learned it's illegal to capture sea lions. If we don't look out for them, who will? They're God's creatures, too."

"If someone stole Mario and Bianca, we need to find out who did it and what they did with the pups," McKenzie said, glancing at her watch. "It's hot out here. Do you want to go back to the beach for a while before Aunt Becca gets off work? That will give us time to figure out how to start this investigation."

Alex agreed as she shut off her camcorder. They

hurried back down the road to the beach house. After grabbing their towels, they headed to the cove. While they were gone, sunbathers had flocked to the beach, spreading out colorful blankets and coolers. Rock music blared out of someone's boom box. A few kites dotted the sky.

McKenzie flung herself onto the sand.

Alex dropped down beside her and stretched out on her stomach with her arms folded beneath her chin. "Isn't it funny that a group of sea lions is called a herd, but baby sea lions are called pups?" Then without waiting for an answer, she asked, "Where should we begin, with this investigation, I mean?"

"Good question." McKenzie started digging in the sand. "We don't know much about the couple that the boy said stole the pups. All we know is that they drove a silver and red boat, and the guy had a fish tattoo. And they had two helpers. Maybe we should try to figure out why someone would want to steal the babies. You're the sea lion expert, Alex. What would someone do with a sea lion?"

Alex thought for a moment, then answered. "Well, it's not to sell the fur, like some animals, because the sea lion doesn't have any fur. Some people in northern Alaska use the skins to make boats, but that would be dumb to steal pups for that."

"That's gross," McKenzie said, making a face. "Surely no one would be mean enough to do that. They wouldn't get much skin out of baby pups, anyway. There must be another reason. Why else would someone want a sea lion?"

"Hmm." Alex wrinkled her brow. "Mario and Bianca were twins, and that's very unusual. Maybe someone wants them for a zoo or something like that."

McKenzie scanned the people lounging on the beach. She wished she would see the mother and her two kids, Keaton and Claire, again. If she did, she would talk to the boy. But she didn't see the family anywhere on this stretch of beach.

"Hey, look." McKenzie nodded in the direction of a boat. "Is that the boat that about ran us over this morning? It kind of looks like the same couple."

Alex turned in the direction McKenzie pointed. "It could be. It all happened so fast that I didn't get a good look at them. But it does look like the boat. It's silver and red, just like the one that kid, Keaton, saw."

The pilot of the boat steered it into the marina and cut the engine. A tall blond woman jumped onto the dock and tied the boat to the dock. They stowed their fishing gear in the back of the boat. Then they each grabbed an end of an old cooler and lugged it onto the dock.

"It is them. That's also the couple that got so mad

because they wanted the Hideaway Bungalow so badly," Alex said.

McKenzie watched the couple carry the cooler across the beach and disappear on a narrow path through the trees. "I'm sure it's them, too."

A figure on the beach caught her attention. "McKenzie! Alex!"

A young woman with short dark hair called and waved at the girls.

"Alex, Aunt Becca's back." McKenzie stood and brushed sand off her legs.

"Hey, girls," Aunt Becca called out as they approached. "How's it going?"

Both girls began talking at the same time, telling Becca about the missing seal pups and the conversation they had overheard with the little boy and his mother.

"And when we were out on the skimmer, a couple that matched that description almost ran us over with their boat, tipping us over and everything," McKenzie explained.

"And then the fog got so bad we could hardly see to get back home. Mr. C. was almost ready to come looking for us," Alex said anxiously.

"What's this?" Aunt Becca frowned at the girls. "You were out and got lost in the fog? How far did you sail?"

"Uh. . ." McKenzie stammered, glancing sheepishly at Alex. "We're not sure. It was so foggy we couldn't see the landmarks."

Uh-oh. We're in trouble now. We've said too much, McKenzie thought. *I've seen that look before.*

Aunt Becca looked from one girl to the other, like she was trying not to get mad. "I know I told you girls you could take the sailboat out, but only if you stayed within a reasonable distance to the beach. You need to stay close enough to land so you can get back safely, even in a fog. I had asked Mr. Carney to keep an eye out for you two. I'm sure he was worried sick."

"We're sorry," both girls said awkwardly.

"Next time you'll need to tell either me or Mr. Carney when you go out. And you definitely need to stay very close. If you got pulled out into the ocean, you'd be in big trouble." Aunt Becca gave them a forced smile.

"Okay, enough of that," she continued. "Now, I'll tell you what I came out here for. How would you like to go flying with me in the Skyview plane? I'm taking a gentleman for a sightseeing tour in about thirty minutes. When I told him about you girls staying with me, he invited you to come along. I talked with my boss, and he said you could ride for free this once, since there's room."

Both girls jumped up and down with excitement as

they hurried to the house. McKenzie couldn't wait to go flying. The girls quickly changed, and Aunt Becca drove the short distance to the small airport.

An older man introduced himself to the girls as Ted Lowry. He climbed into the front seat beside Aunt Becca. The girls settled into the backseat and fastened their seat belts. Aunt Becca taxied down the runway and expertly lifted the plane into the air.

"Yeee-iiikes!" McKenzie clutched her stomach as the plane climbed higher and higher. McKenzie had ridden in jets but never in a small plane like this. She felt weightless, sailing through the air. When Aunt Becca swooped low, McKenzie felt she was on an amusement ride.

Aunt Becca flew the plane along the coast, shouting above the roar of the engine, "You'll see the city of Florence to your right. The Emerald Bay Resort is just below us. You can see our cabin, girls, next to Mr. C.'s. Then the Hideaway Cabin is behind all those trees."

That's the Frankses' cabin, McKenzie thought. *Why would anyone want to stay in a cabin hidden in the woods like that? It's so isolated, no one would even know it's there.*

"Look at the people on the beach," McKenzie said, nudging Alex. "They look like tiny little bugs, and the homes and stores looked like miniature dollhouses.

This is so cool!"

Aunt Becca flew the plane up and down the coast, pointing out various points of interest. "Cape Perpetua and the Heceta Head Lighthouse are just ahead a few miles," she said.

All too soon, the flight was over and Aunt Becca landed the Skyview back on the runway. After they had taxied to the hangar, she cut the engine.

Mr. Lowry turned around in his seat to face the girls. "Becca here tells me you two are working on a special report on sea lions for your public TV station. That is quite an honor, McKenzie."

McKenzie felt her face flush as she thanked him.

He cleared his throat and continued. "I'm retired from the University of Oregon. I've spent years doing research on Steller sea lions. Tomorrow I'm going out on a boat with a crew that is training sea lions for use in government operations. I've already talked with Becca. She has given me permission to ask a favor of you girls."

McKenzie looked at Alex. "Okay," she stammered.

The older man grinned. "Don't look so worried. It's not every day kids your age get to ride along on one of these training sessions."

McKenzie stared at him as her pulse quickened. *Did I hear him right? Is he really asking us to come with him?*

"Are you serious?" she stammered.

Mr. Lowry chuckled. "Of course. I'm officially inviting you to be my guests. So, how about it? How would you girls like to go with me on the boat and videotape the crew as they work with the sea lions?"

McKenzie noticed that Alex looked as excited as she was.

How lucky can we get? McKenzie thought. *Maybe, just maybe, he can help us find Mario and Bianca!*

A Scream in the Night

For a minute McKenzie didn't know what to say. She still couldn't believe Mr. Lowry was serious.

McKenzie turned to Alex who was nodding, her dark ponytail bouncing up and down. "Well, sure. I mean, thank you, Mr. Lowry."

"Then it's all settled. I'll drop by about seven thirty tomorrow morning. We'll head to the port and meet the rest of the crew there."

The girls climbed out of the airplane and said good-bye to Mr. Lowry. They chatted excitedly on the drive back to the beach house. The sailing trip tomorrow would give them a great chance to film the report.

When McKenzie went to bed that night, scattered thoughts filled her mind. *I can't believe we're going in the sea with Mr. Lowry tomorrow. Hopefully we can get some great video footage of the sea lions.* She finally fell asleep to the sound of the waves rolling onto the beach.

—•—

McKenzie was the first one up in the morning. She woke Alex and by seven thirty, both girls were waiting outside when Mr. Lowry pulled up in his red pickup truck. They hollered good-bye to Aunt Becca and climbed into the car. Twenty minutes later, he pulled into a parking spot at the port.

"What are we going to do today?" McKenzie asked after the three climbed aboard the largest boat at the docks.

Mr. Lowry pointed at a vessel out a little way in the Pacific Ocean. "That ship belongs to the United States Navy. The navy has trained sea lions to protect U.S. ships from underwater terrorists. In their mouths, these sea lions carry a clamp that is attached to a rope. They fasten that to the leg of any diver approaching a ship. The sailors on the ship can then pull the person from the water."

"What does that have to do with us?" McKenzie asked.

"After we approach the ship, one of our men will dive into the water to test the sea lions," Mr. Lowry explained. "You girls will want to have your camera going. You should get some good footage."

Mr. Lowry handed each girl a life jacket. "I'll introduce you to our crew."

He called to a man in a blue jacket sitting behind the steering wheel. "Hey, Warren, I'd like you to meet my young friends, McKenzie Phillips and Alexis Howell. They're here to film a report for Montana Public TV."

The girls chatted with the captain. Then Mr. Lowry led them to the back of the boat where two more men waited. A blond-haired man, wearing a black scuba diving suit, turned as the girls approached. He shook the girls' hands and introduced himself as Josh.

The other man had dark hair and wore swimming trunks and a long-sleeved T-shirt. He ignored the girls as he focused binoculars on the navy ship. After a few seconds he turned to meet the girls.

McKenzie felt her jaw drop. Before she could speak, Mr. Lowry said, "McKenzie, Alex, I'd like you to meet Mel Franks, our sea lion expert and head diver today."

For a minute, McKenzie thought Mr. Franks wasn't going to respond. He stared at one girl and then the other, a crease forming on his forehead. *I wonder if he knows we're the ones he almost clobbered yesterday with his boat.*

"Nice to meet you, Mr. Franks," McKenzie said as she stuck out her hand.

He hesitated but shook her hand. He looked at her, as if he couldn't figure out where he'd seen her. McKenzie didn't know what to say or do. She didn't really want to ask him why he had almost flattened them.

Mel Franks glanced at his wristwatch and turned to Mr. Lowry. "Ted, why don't you go tell Tony to fire up the engine? It's time to move on."

The moment Mr. Lowry stepped away, Mr. Franks turned to the girls. "Didn't I see you girls out in the cove yesterday?"

McKenzie and Alex glanced sheepishly at each other. "Yes, our sailboat tipped," McKenzie explained. She left out the part that he was responsible for capsizing them.

"You girls stay away from that area. It's too dangerous in there, with all the rocks and churning waters. That can pull you right down. I can't believe your parents let you go out there," Mr. Franks scolded.

"Our parents aren't here," McKenzie said. "We're staying with my aunt in the Seaside Bungalow."

Mel Franks glanced around at the blond-haired man looking their way, then muttered, "Well, see to it that you stay away from that area, or I'll have a talk with your aunt."

McKenzie took a step backward, wishing Mr. Lowry would return. She sighed with relief when the boat's motor rumbled to life, and the older man appeared.

"Hey, Mel," Mr. Lowry called. "Aren't you going

down first? You'd better suit up."

"Yeah, yeah, I'm going," Mr. Franks said, suddenly in a lighthearted mood. He peeled off his shirt and strode to the back of the boat.

McKenzie stifled a gasp. She couldn't believe her eyes. She nudged Alex and nodded at the blue and green fish tattoo on Mel's arm!

Mr. Franks glared at her and slipped into his scuba suit. Alex opened her mouth to speak, but McKenzie shook her head. Her heart raced as she watched Mel.

"Come on up here with your camera, girls." Mr. Lowry motioned as the motorboat approached the navy ship. "Mel's going down. Then you'll see the sea lions go to work."

McKenzie wanted to talk privately with Alex but knew she couldn't do that while they were on the boat. *What is going on?* she wondered. *Is Mr. Franks the man that boy saw steal Mario and Bianca?*

When the boat was about fifty yards from the ship, Tony cut the boat's engine. A message crackled over his two-way radio. He spoke into the mouthpiece and turned to the crew on deck. "Captain said, 'anytime now.'"

With his breathing gear in place, Mr. Franks flipped backward off the side of the boat. McKenzie saw the outline of his body as he swam toward the ship.

"See the sea lion." Mr. Lowry pointed at a dark

shadow beneath the water. "It's swimming to Mr. Franks with the clamp in its mouth. Watch what happens next."

McKenzie lost sight of Mel. Seconds later, the rope hanging over the side of the navy ship jerked. The crew onboard the ship quickly reeled in Mr. Franks, hanging upside down with his leg attached to a rope. McKenzie laughed. Mr. Franks looked so funny as the navy guys hauled him onto the deck.

The rest of the crew cheered, declaring the practice mission a success. Then Josh took his turn diving. This time Alex filmed McKenzie explaining the role sea lions played in the military. In the background, Alex filmed Josh as he was jerked from the water.

They waited until a motorboat taxied Mr. Franks and Josh back to Mr. Lowry's boat. After the two men climbed aboard, Tony headed back to shore. Since these men knew a lot about sea lions, McKenzie asked the question that had been bugging her all morning.

"Mr. Lowry, have you heard about the twin sea lion pups that are missing?" She had to almost shout to be heard over the roar of the engine.

Mel Franks turned sharply, shooting McKenzie an angry look. Mr. Lowry didn't seem to notice as he offered the girls cold drinks from a cooler.

"Yes, I heard about that. I've heard talk that

poachers got them," the older man said sadly.

"I'm guessing killer whales got them," Mel Franks said. "Poachers wouldn't have any use for sea lion pups."

Mr. Franks changed the subject back to the sea lion mission they had just finished. McKenzie's suspicions about him began to grow. He sure fit the description of the man the little boy had seen. And he obviously didn't want to talk about Mario and Bianca. *If he did steal them, why would he do it? If he's an expert on sea lions, surely he would want to keep them safe, though,* McKenzie thought.

The crew quickly arrived back in port. The girls thanked Mr. Lowry for letting them tag along. McKenzie noticed that everyone seemed happy they had come. Everyone, except for Mel Franks.

—•—•—•—

"Aunt Becca, may we use your computer to chat with the Camp Club Girls?" McKenzie asked.

"Sure. Is that the group of girls you met at camp awhile back?" Aunt Becca opened the refrigerator door and surveyed its contents.

"Yes, we have so much fun." McKenzie led the way to the computer.

"We're also really good at solving mysteries," Alex piped up. "We're going to try to figure out what happened to Mario and Bianca."

"That could be a tough job," Aunt Becca said, preheating the oven for a frozen pan of lasagna. "Lots of things could have happened to them. I know it's not a nice thought, but sea lions have natural predators. Like sharks and killer whales."

"That's what Mr. Franks said, too. But would an animal get both of them at the same time?" McKenzie logged on to the computer.

Aunt Becca shrugged. "I'm surprised Mr. Franks was on the boat this morning. He's one of Emerald Bay's regular customers."

McKenzie decided it was time to tell Aunt Becca everything they knew. "We heard a little boy on the beach say he saw a man and a woman steal Mario and Bianca yesterday morning. He said the man had a fish tattoo on his arm." She paused for a moment before continuing. "Mr. Franks has a tattoo just like that."

Aunt Becca looked startled. "I can't imagine why Mel Franks would steal sea lions. I know you girls like to solve mysteries, but when it involves other people, you have to be extra careful. After all, you didn't see the man steal anything. And remember to talk to God first before doing anything that might hurt someone."

"Oh, we will," Alex said as she pulled a chair up beside McKenzie. "That's one reason we like to talk to the other Camp Club Girls. We always pray for each other and help each other."

"Okay. I'll trust you girls to do the right thing. I guess I'm as curious as you are about those pups," Aunt Becca said before slipping out the front door with a book.

Mickey lay at the girls' feet as they signed in to the chat room. McKenzie told the girls about the conversation they had overheard on the beach earlier. Then McKenzie told them all about Mr. Franks capsizing their sailboat yesterday and the discovery of the cave on the inlet. She continued by sharing the news of their outing earlier that day with Mr. Lowry and his crew.

Bailey: *Maybe Mr. . .uh. . .what's his name. . .the cave man guy wanted to go to the cave and you were in his way.*

Sydney: *You mean, Mr. Franks? I don't know why he tipped McKenzie and Alex's sailboat, but we do have some clues already about the kidnappers. We know it was a man with a fish tattoo and a woman. Mr. Franks has a tattoo like that, but some other guy could have one, too.*

Elizabeth: *That's right. But don't forget the silver and red boat.*

Kate: *You'll have to find the pups before you can*

prove anything. Can you watch for silver and red boats in the area? If that couple stole two pups, they might be back for more.

McKenzie: *That would be good, Kate. But maybe we can watch Mr. and Mrs. Franks closely and find out what is going on.*

Sydney: *Sea lions, like all animals, do best in natural surroundings. Maybe the kidnappers took them to a natural environment somewhere to care for them, like a zoo.*

The Camp Club Girls discussed the disappearance awhile longer. Before signing off, McKenzie promised to keep them posted with any new information about the investigation.

After supper McKenzie and Alex stepped outside with their cameras. Sunset was near. Alex hoped to get some pictures of bounding whales for the photography contest. As they approached the dock, Mr. Carney called to them from his backyard.

"Hey, Mr. C.," McKenzie hollered, scurrying toward the older man sitting in his lawn chair reading in the fading light.

"I've been reading this book on local caves you picked up for me yesterday," he said as he snapped the book shut. "It's fascinating. According to the author, several little-known caves are on the Oregon coast. A couple of them are right around here."

"Really? Where?" McKenzie asked excitedly.

"I'm just getting to that part, but it's about too dark to read. Besides, I need to go in the house and finish packing my bag." He paused. "My son is taking me to his home. I won't be back until later tomorrow. I might have a few minutes to read before he gets here. Why don't I loan the book to you when I get back?"

The girls eagerly agreed and then headed to the dock. Alex took several pictures of the western sky, painted with streaks of pink, orange, and blue. McKenzie sat on the dock, dangling her legs over the side. She kicked her feet in the cool, clear water. Alex lowered her camera and pointed out a family of loons gliding through the shadowy water of the cove.

"Do you think Mel and Tia Franks stole the sea lion pups?" Alex asked as she sat down cross-legged beside McKenzie.

"I don't know. The evidence sure points to them." McKenzie scratched her arm. "That is, if we can believe the story that little boy told."

Alex sighed. "I wish we had seen the couple in the boat that morning. We only have a rumor to go on. We can't accuse anyone based on that."

McKenzie jumped as her cell phone rang. She

pulled it from her pocket and flipped it open. "Hey, Sydney," she said after recognizing her friend's phone number. "What's up?"

"When Bailey called Mr. Franks 'Cave Man,' I started thinking. Maybe Mr. Franks tipped your sailboat over on purpose yesterday."

"Why would he do that?" McKenzie pulled her feet out of the water and tucked her wet legs beneath her.

"He tipped you over by the cave entrance, right? Maybe he didn't want you to see something in that cave, like nets or something. I don't know how anyone steals a sea lion, but maybe there's stuff in there they use to capture sea mammals. If they stole two sea lions, they might steal more," Sydney explained.

McKenzie thought for a moment. "I didn't see anything in the cave. Except for a little bit of trash."

"I thought if the thieves stole two pups, they might come back for more. I mean, who would know if any other sea lion pups were missing? If Susie wasn't such a favorite for tourists, who would know Mario and Bianca were missing?" Sydney continued.

"I guess you've got a point," McKenzie answered. "But there's no way we can go back to the cave. Aunt Becca would never let us sail back over there."

"Oh, well. It was just an idea," Sydney said. "I'm just looking for clues."

By the time McKenzie hung up the phone, darkness had settled in and a cool wind had come up. A full moon and a sprinkling of stars lit up the sky. The lights of the resorts farther down the beach dotted the shoreline. Talking about Mr. Franks and his strange behavior on Mr. Lowry's boat made her feel uneasy. All the talk about thieves, missing sea lions, and dark caves made her shiver.

"Let's go in," McKenzie said as she stood and headed toward the light glowing in the kitchen window of the beach house.

"Good idea," Alex said, in close pursuit. "I need a snack before bed, anyway."

Hurrying up the sidewalk leading to the house, McKenzie set her camera on the porch railing. She kicked off her flip-flops and turned on the outside faucet. Then she stuck her foot under the stream of water to rinse the sand off her feet.

She jerked herself upright and froze in horror as a crazy, laughlike scream pierced the night!

The Intruder!

A feeling like icy cold fingers rippled up McKenzie's neck as she lunged through the doorway. "What was that?" Her voice trembled as she turned to Alex.

A look of shock passed over Alex's face, then she giggled. "You should see the look on your face. That's just a loon calling for its mate."

McKenzie's face grew warm, and her breathing began to return to normal. "You mean that was a bird? It sounded like a maniac laughing and screaming at the same time."

"Oooh-ooh-ooh-OOOH!" Alex let out a mournful cry. She raised her arms high and bent her fingers like crooked claws. "I'm a scary loon, and I'm going to get you."

McKenzie playfully punched her friend in the arm. "That's the creepiest-sounding bird I've ever heard. It sounded like a scream."

"It used to scare me, too," Alex said, grabbing a box of cheesy crackers from a kitchen cupboard. "But now

I love to hear the loons calling to each other."

McKenzie shivered as the loon's cry carried through the open windows of the sun porch. She rubbed her arms to chase away the chill. As she reached for the light switch, something warm and fuzzy brushed against her leg.

"Aaaahhh!" she screeched, jumping as something cold and wet touched her hand.

Glancing down, she sighed with relief. "Oh, Mickey. I'm glad it's you, boy." She patted the dog's head as he danced about her feet, whimpering.

"I think he needs to go out," Alex said, bending to scratch Mickey's ears. She held out a couple of crackers and dropped them, letting the dog catch them in his mouth. Then she reached up and grabbed a leash from a hook by the back door.

"You don't mean we're going back out there, do you?" McKenzie asked, feeling like a scaredy-cat.

"Aah, come with me." Alex snapped the leash onto the dog's collar. "Let's just take Mickey out for a minute."

McKenzie hesitated, but then followed Alex and Mickey out the door into the cool night air. The glow of the yard lights in front of each cabin lined the beach like a string of Christmas lights. The dog scampered about their feet, tugging the leash until Alex was almost running to keep up.

McKenzie scurried after them until Mickey stopped at the nearest tree and sniffed. Though the loons still called their eerie cry in the distance, she wasn't as scared as she had been earlier. *It still sounds creepy, but at least I know it's just a bird*, she thought.

"Uh-oh," Alex said, looking at McKenzie as she tugged on the leash. "What time is it?"

"Five after ten," McKenzie said after pushing the tiny button on the side of her watch so it would light up.

"I told Mom and Dad I'd call them at ten. I'd better do that now." Alex handed McKenzie the leash. "I'll be right back."

Alex sped toward the back steps and let the screen door bang behind her. McKenzie let Mickey pull her toward the next tree. *Come on, dog. Hurry up and do your business. I don't like it out here alone.*

McKenzie glanced around. The cabin to her right stood in darkness. Apparently the renters staying there weren't home yet for the night. She turned toward Mr. Carney's cabin on the other side of Aunt Becca's cabin. The dark windows reminded her that the older man was spending the night with his son.

Her gaze continued to the left, noting the dark grove of pine trees standing like a black forest separating Mr. Carney's cabin from the Hideaway.

McKenzie had never seen the Hideaway except from Aunt Becca's airplane. Tucked behind the grove of trees, it was completely hidden from view. A maintenance road behind the cabins was the only entrance to the isolated cabin. Even then it was a quarter of a mile hike from the road to the Hideaway.

Mickey tugged McKenzie around the tree, sniffing the ground. An owl hooted somewhere in the top of a nearby tree. The wind whistled through the pine needles. McKenzie shivered while she watched Alex through the window, talking on the phone with her parents.

"Okay, Mickey," she muttered as she tied the dog's leash around a tree trunk. "I'm not waiting out here all night. It's too creepy out here for me. I'll be back in a few minutes."

McKenzie sprinted up the back steps and into the house, feeling like the biggest chicken ever. Normally, the dark didn't bother her, but too many weird sounds were freaking her out. Sounds she wasn't used to.

Once inside, she relaxed and grabbed a handful of peanuts from a bowl on the coffee table. She settled onto the arm of the couch. Alex smiled and kept chatting into the phone's receiver.

Aunt Becca walked into the family room, wearing a purple terry-cloth bathrobe. She hugged McKenzie and whispered, "I'm going to bed. I've got to be at work early in the morning. Don't stay up too late."

McKenzie returned her hug and said, "Good night." Aunt Becca gave Alex a quick squeeze and went down the hall to her bedroom.

After Alex hung up, McKenzie stood and wiped her hands on her jeans. "Finally," she teased. "We'd better go get Mickey. He probably thinks we forgot him."

The girls scurried out the back door and raced down the steps. Moonlight flickered through the branches that rustled in the night. Gentle rolling waves in the cove lapped upon the beach. A screen door slammed shut somewhere down the beach, and a shadowy couple walked across the moonlit sand. The cluster of torchlights in front of the resort looked like tiny dots flickering in the wind.

"Where did you leave him?" Alex asked, interrupting McKenzie's thoughts.

McKenzie pointed at a tree bathed in the glow of the yard light. "Right there, next to the hammock."

"I don't see him," Alex said as she squinted into the darkness.

McKenzie ran toward the tree. *I'm sure this is where I left the dog.* "Oh, great! His leash must have come untied. Where did he go?"

"Here, Mickey!" Alex called, looking toward the

beach and then back to the yard. "Here, boy."

McKenzie whistled. She paused and listened but didn't hear an answering bark. *Mickey, why did you have to run off?* she asked silently, glancing about for any sign of the dog.

The girls searched the yard, peering behind every shrub and tree. McKenzie had an uneasy feeling. Soon all she could hear was the loud thumping in her chest.

"We need a flashlight," Alex said, darting back inside the house.

Shivering as she waited on the back steps, McKenzie felt the cool breeze cut through her shirt. She considered going after a sweatshirt, but Alex bounded out the door and down the steps.

"Where should we look?" McKenzie asked, following her friend.

"How about that way?" Alex pointed toward Mr. Carney's yard. The yard light by the beach shone through the tree branches, casting eerie shadows on the ground.

Scritch! Scratch! The branches scraped against the metal light pole. Alex switched on the flashlight as the girls stepped across the yard. She shined the light around Mr. Carney's porch and peeked behind the bushes out front.

"Do you see him?" McKenzie whispered, peering

over her friend's shoulder.

"No, but I did find this." Alex bent and picked up an object caught on the bush.

"That's Mickey's leash. He must have been caught and worked it loose." McKenzie frowned as she took the leash and wrapped it around her hand. "At least we know we're headed in the right direction."

Taking a deep breath, McKenzie huddled close to Alex. They crossed Mr. Carney's yard and approached the grove of trees. Wind whistled through the needles of the pines, standing like an army waiting to attack. Crickets chirped and bullfrogs croaked. A large bird swooped down from out of nowhere. And, of course, the crazy loons were still at it, making the hair on the back of McKenzie's neck twitch.

I know now why people who want a secluded cabin would come to this resort, McKenzie thought. *I'm glad our cabin is closer to the lodge where there are more people around.*

McKenzie felt a chill run up her back. She couldn't help feeling like Dorothy in *The Wizard of Oz.*

I'd better not see any flying monkeys, she thought with a tremble. She remembered how that part of the movie had terrified her when she was little.

She eyed the grove as if someone might be hiding there now. Every stump and shadow beckoned eerily.

The sweet, tangy scent of the pine trees wafted over her in the night air. A faint whimper came from somewhere deep in the grove.

"I hear something." McKenzie paused and then called softly, just in case someone else was listening nearby. "Mickey, here boy."

Again, she heard the faintest whimpering cry. She clutched Alex's arm. "Did you hear that?"

"Yes. We'd better go look for him," Alex said, pointing the beam of light into the darkness.

Hanging on to each other, the girls stepped into the shadows. They ducked beneath branches as they called Mickey's name. Pine needles stung McKenzie in the face, and her shirt caught on a bramble. She tugged it loose and hurried onward.

She knew they had to be getting close to the Hideaway. When they came to the yard of the last cabin, the small, boxlike cottage stood dark and lifeless. McKenzie knew why it was given the name Hideaway. It was completely hidden from the rest of the cabins and the main stretch of beach. The moonlight shining on the windowpanes stared at her like glassy eyes. Once she thought she saw a flash of light inside, but when she looked again, everything was dark.

"So this is where the Frankses are staying?" Alex asked, pointing the flashlight at the house.

"Yeah, but shut your light off. There's enough moonlight coming through the trees so we can see without it," McKenzie whispered. "I don't think anybody's home, but if they are, I don't want to get caught out here."

McKenzie tipped her head as another whimper carried on the wind. "I heard it again!" McKenzie said. "It sounded like it came from over there—past the house."

Pulling Alex with her, McKenzie raced past the screened-in porch on the cabin to a cluster of bushes hugging the far side of the yard. A *yip* sounded—closer this time.

"Shine your light back here." McKenzie turned to Alex and knelt beside the shrubs.

McKenzie felt something wet on her arm as two beady eyes shined in the flashlight beam. A long slobbery tongue hung from a gaping mouth.

"Mickey!" Alex cried. "Oh, look, McKenzie. His collar's caught on a branch."

While Alex held the flashlight, McKenzie quickly untangled the dog. He jumped the moment he was free, yipping and licking the girls' faces. Despite being scared, she couldn't help but giggle with relief that they had found Mickey.

McKenzie clipped the leash back on the collar and

pulled the dog from his hiding spot. "We need to get out of here before the Frankses get home."

"Yeah, I'm never going to get to sleep tonight. I'm too antsy. I wish I had a good book to read. I only brought one with me, and I'm almost done with it," Alex said, clicking the flashlight off again and stepping away from the bushes. "Too bad Mr. C. didn't give us that book before he left. I'm dying to find out where those caves are around here."

"Me, too." McKenzie tugged Mickey's leash as they walked back across the Frankses' yard. "Maybe we could go exploring, but definitely in the daylight."

When they approached the dark grove of trees, the squeak of a screen door cut through the night. McKenzie froze and turned slowly toward the Frankses' sun porch. She saw nothing, but heard muffled voices from inside the house. Then all was silent again.

Had someone been on the screened-in sun porch all along? One of the voices sure sounded like Mrs. Franks, McKenzie thought anxiously. *And both voices sounded like women.*

McKenzie felt her pulse quicken. Alex stood motionless beside her. Grasping Alex's arm, McKenzie ran through the trees, pulling Mickey with her. The branches tore at her hair, and pine needles scratched her arm. They sped through the grove. The beam from Alex's flashlight bobbed up and down wildly as they dodged the maze of trees.

After darting across Mr. Carney's yard, the girls arrived, breathless, at their back porch. Once inside, McKenzie unhooked Mickey's leash. He trotted eagerly to his bowl in the kitchen and slurped the water.

"That was so-o-o weird!" Alex said after catching her breath. "Was Mrs. Franks watching and listening to us the whole time we were in her yard?"

McKenzie grabbed a tissue and dabbed at a bleeding scratch on her arm. "I don't know for sure, but I think she and someone else must have been out there."

"Why wouldn't she let us know she was there? It's almost like she was spying on us," Alex said while handing Mickey a dog biscuit.

McKenzie didn't answer. *It does seem like she was spying, but why?* Though McKenzie's breath had returned to normal, she still felt nervous. *God, forgive me if I'm wrong to suspect the Frankses, but something just doesn't seem right. I'm scared,* McKenzie quietly prayed.

Mickey settled onto his pillow in the corner of the kitchen. The girls headed down the hall to their bedroom. As McKenzie was about to slip under the covers, she suddenly remembered she had left her camera on the railing outside earlier in the evening.

"I'll be right back," she said to Alex and scurried down the dark hallway to the back door. With the moonlight shining through the window, she didn't need to turn on any lights. She quickly opened the door and grabbed the camera. As she turned to step back inside, she glanced toward Mr. Carney's cabin.

Was somebody on Mr. C.'s sun porch?

McKenzie slipped back into the shadows. The figure moved into the moonlight, bending over as if picking something up off the floor. Then the figure stepped back into the darkness. Someone, a woman, had just come out of Mr. Carney's cabin and was standing on the sun porch!

The Empty Cabin

McKenzie raced back into the bedroom she shared with Alex. "Someone is in Mr. Carney's house!"

Alex sat cross-legged in bed, wearing a pair of pink and blue polka-dot pajamas. She put down the mystery she was reading. She looked stunned at her friend's outburst. "Are you sure?"

"Positive." McKenzie felt her heart racing. "I saw her in the moonlight, standing on the sun porch."

Alex flung the covers back and jumped out of bed. "What do we do now?"

Without hesitation, McKenzie answered, "We'd better wake Aunt Becca. She'll know what to do."

McKenzie knocked on her aunt's bedroom door and flung the door wide open. The hall light spilled onto Aunt Becca's form lying on the bed.

"What's up, girls?" Aunt Becca said with a yawn as she rolled over, squinting at the bright light.

"There's a robber in Mr. C.'s cabin," Alex blurted out.

"What's this?" Aunt Becca swung her legs over the side of the bed and sat up. "What makes you think that?"

"I saw a woman on the porch," McKenzie explained, rushing her words. "I saw her, just now."

Aunt Becca slipped out of bed and scurried into the dark family room. Standing near the window, she peered cautiously toward the neighboring cabin. "I don't see anyone," she whispered.

"She must have left already," McKenzie spoke softly. "But someone was there. I saw her, plain as day. . .or night, whatever."

Aunt Becca moved quickly into the kitchen and switched on the light. "I really don't want to call the police. There could be a logical explanation for this. I think Mr. Carney gave me his son's phone number once. I'll try to find it and call him before it gets any later. I hate to worry him. But if someone is prowling, he needs to know."

Aunt Becca located the phone number and paced the room nervously after dialing. Moments later, McKenzie could tell that Mr. Carney's son had answered. Aunt Becca explained the situation. After a slight pause, she thanked the man and hung up.

"Well, you girls can sleep peacefully tonight. Al, Mr. C.'s son, said his dad had been having problems with his Internet. So he had asked the resort to send over a technician while he was gone. That must have been who you saw."

McKenzie looked quizzically at Alex. "What a weird time for someone to fix it."

"Mr. C. is a good, regular customer of Emerald Bay. He comes here every summer. If he wanted his Internet restored by the time he returns, I'm sure the staff would fix it." Aunt Becca seemed to accept the explanation without question. "They have a computer person on staff who probably just didn't get to it earlier today." With a yawn and a wave, she headed back down the hall.

McKenzie felt more relaxed since Aunt Becca had made the phone call, but something just didn't seem right. If the woman on the sun porch was working on a computer, wouldn't she be carrying some kind of bag or briefcase? But the woman McKenzie had seen wasn't carrying anything, at least nothing very big.

"That doesn't make any sense," McKenzie said. "Why would a repair person stand in the dark on the sun porch like she was trying to hide? I think something is going on over there."

●—●—●

When the girls awoke the next morning, Aunt Becca had already left for work. As they ate breakfast, McKenzie suggested that they tour the Sea Lion Harbor later in the day. She wanted to get some more footage of sea lions for her video report. By the end of the week, she would be on a plane back to Montana.

As the girls loaded the dishwasher, they heard a knock at the front door. A man wearing a brown uniform stood in the doorway with a package and an electronic clipboard.

McKenzie opened the door, and the man smiled at her. "I have a package for Mr. Lon Carney, but no one is home. My note says that it can be left with his neighbor. Could I get you to sign for me, please? Then I'll leave the package here with you."

"Sure," McKenzie said, signing her name on the pad.

The man handed her the package, thanked her, and went back to his truck. McKenzie watched the truck disappear down a bend in the road.

"Why don't we take this package over to Mr. C.'s house now and leave it on his porch?" McKenzie suggested. "We might not be here when he gets home this afternoon, and he might want it before we get back."

"Sounds good to me," Alex agreed while she wiped off the countertop.

A few moments later, the girls walked up the back steps of Mr. Carney's sun porch. Like McKenzie figured, the door was unlocked. They slipped inside and set the package by the door leading into his cabin.

McKenzie's mind went to the woman she had seen standing here last night. McKenzie glanced around the sun porch. She had only been here one other time, when she and Alex had brought the cave book over. But something seemed out of place. *What was different?*

She glanced at the little family of wooden loons clustered by the back door. She knew the loons had been lined up neatly when she had been here before.

Lots of people hide a spare key by the back door, she thought.

Instinctively, she picked up the largest loon and looked beneath it. A piece of clear tape hung loosely to the bottom.

She reached over to the middle-sized loon. Beneath it was a house key on the ground. It was the same size as the tape.

"Something is definitely not right, Alex. It looks like Mr. C. kept a spare key taped to the bottom of this loon. But it also looks like someone took the key and put it back under the wrong loon. And why would the resort staff need his key? Wouldn't they have their own?"

"Yes." Alex nodded. "But how would a thief know where Mr. C. kept his key?"

"She could have guessed. Lots of people hide their spare keys close to the door." McKenzie scratched at a mosquito bite on her arm.

"I guess that's true," Alex said with a sigh. "So, now what do we do? Aunt Becca and Mr. C. think a computer techie went into his cabin, but we think it was a robber."

McKenzie sighed and glanced out the screened-in porch. "I guess we'll have to wait until Mr. C. comes home and then tell him what we've found, and see if anything was stolen. I don't want to bother Aunt Becca about it at work. I didn't get a good look at the woman because it was so dark. But I think she was young."

"Did she look like Mrs. Franks?" Alex asked.

"A little bit. She was about her height, but I don't think it was her. It was dark, but I think she had short blond hair. Mrs. Franks has long hair." McKenzie shoved the loons back in place and stood up.

"Maybe she had her hair in a ponytail," Alex suggested.

"That's possible," McKenzie said.

After returning home, the girls spent the rest of the morning flying a bright, sea lion-shaped kite and hunting for seashells. They wanted to hang around the house so they could talk to Mr. Carney the minute he got home.

Soon after lunch, McKenzie heard a car door slam and voices outside Mr. Carney's cabin. She pulled the curtain back and glanced out the window as a black car pulled away from the cabin.

"Mr. C.'s home." McKenzie turned to Alex. "Let's go talk to him about the woman we saw last night."

Minutes later the girls stood on their neighbor's porch, knocking on the door.

"Well, well." Mr. Carney answered the door with a smile. "It's good to see you girls. I appreciate you keeping an eye on things for me last night. It's nice to know someone's watching out for me while I'm gone."

"That's what we wanted to talk to you about," McKenzie said. "We think things look suspicious."

"Suspicious?" Mr. Carney frowned as he ushered the girls inside. "How?"

Both girls began talking at once. They told him about finding the spare key, the wadded-up piece of tape, and the misplaced wooden loons.

"Whoa, whoa, wait a minute. What's this about finding my spare key?"

McKenzie tugged his arm, leading him onto the sun porch. "We brought a package over for you this morning. I thought something looked strange, and I realized the wooden loons were out of order. They're always nice and neat. Then I saw the corner of the spare key sticking out from under one of them."

"We think someone found your spare key and went inside your cabin last night," Alex explained. "Then she got in a hurry and put it back under the wrong loon. You do hide a key there, don't you?"

Mr. Carney scratched his head. "I do hide it under the first loon. I reckon it's probably a little too obvious."

He paused, then continued, "Let me check inside. I'll see if anything is missing."

The girls followed him into the family room and waited on the couch. Mr. Carney went down the hallway and disappeared into a room.

A few minutes later he returned. "Nothing seems to be missing. I have no cash to speak of in the cabin. Did you see this woman carrying anything out?"

McKenzie met Alex's gaze. "I don't think so. Unless it was small and she hid it under her jacket."

"Well, I do know the resort staff came over sometime after I left last night. My Internet is running. Could you have just seen the computer repair lady?"

"But McKenzie saw her bend down, like she was putting something on the floor by the back door," Alex reasoned. "Maybe she was putting the key back."

Mr. Carney smiled at the girls. "She probably accidently kicked the loons and bent over to shove them aside."

Hmm, McKenzie thought with a frown. *That makes sense. But there could still be a clue here. And I don't want to miss it.*

"I have an idea," McKenzie announced. "Why don't you call the resort office and ask them what time the computer techie came over? Then we'd know if it was the resort staff or someone else."

"Or Mrs. Franks," Alex piped in, hopping to her feet.

"Tia Franks?" Mr. Carney asked. "Is that who you thought you saw last night?"

McKenzie glanced at Alex, then turned back to her neighbor. "Well, it kind of looked like her, but her hair was different. Do you know her?"

"Everyone around here knows Mel and Tia Franks. She would have no reason to break into my cabin, girls." Mr. Carney smiled gently at them. "The Frankses are wealthy. They've done extensive research on sea lions and caves in the area. They're very well known in their field. I have nothing that would be of value to them. Besides, I see nothing out of place in here."

McKenzie began to feel a little foolish. Had she just imagined that the woman looked a little like Mrs. Franks?

"I'll tell you what. I'll go ahead and call the resort office to see if they keep a record of times their staff makes calls." Mr. Carney picked up his phone on the end table and punched in a few numbers.

He spoke to someone on the other end of the line for a few minutes and then hung up. "They don't keep track of the time service calls are made. All they know is a young female staff member got the Internet running last evening sometime."

McKenzie was beginning to wish she had never seen the woman. She felt there was something suspicious, but she couldn't prove it. *Why were there no lights on in the cabin when I saw her, not even on the sun porch? Because she didn't want to be seen, that's why!*

"I'm sorry we bothered you, Mr. C. Maybe I was mistaken," McKenzie said. "She just acted so. . .funny, you know?"

Mr. Carney put his arms around McKenzie's and Alex's shoulders. "Don't worry about it, girls. Like I said earlier, I'm glad you're looking out for me." He paused. "Hey, I was going to loan you that book about caves before you leave. I haven't finished it, but I'll let you read about the local caves. Let me get it."

The girls waited as Mr. Carney headed to his bedroom. After a few minutes, he returned. "I can't seem to find it. I thought I left it on the nightstand, but I'll have to look around for it and bring it over later."

As the girls headed to the back door, McKenzie turned to her neighbor. "I've been wondering. If Mr. and Mrs. Franks are so rich, why are they staying at this resort? There are a lot fancier resorts than this one."

"They come to this cabin every summer while they

do work with the Sea Park and other sea lion projects. It's isolated and quieter than any other resort," Mr. Carney answered.

The girls told their neighbor good-bye and headed back to their own yard. They plunked down into the hammock, swinging it back and forth.

"Do you think we'll find out what happened to Mario and Bianca?" Alex asked as she pulled on a hangnail and made it bleed. "Or do you think it's too late. . .if you know what I mean."

McKenzie cringed at the thought. "I can't believe Mario and Bianca are dead. Surely God wouldn't let that happen to them, would He?"

"I sure hope not," Alex said glumly. "But it seems that some people are just born nasty."

"I know. But I don't think it's a coincidence that Mario and Bianca disappeared while we were out here doing a video report on sea lions. I think God allowed all this to happen so we can figure out what happened to them."

"Maybe," Alex said as she wrapped the hem of her blue T-shirt around her bleeding finger. "Maybe we could go look around the resort lobby sometime and see if there's an employee who looks like the woman you saw on the sun porch. At least then we'd know if it was Mrs. Franks or not."

"That's a good idea. And I've also been thinking," McKenzie said, chewing her bottom lip. "Maybe Mrs. Franks, or whoever that lady was, stole Mr. C.'s book on caves. He said he couldn't find it, and he was sure he left it on his nightstand."

"But he also said the Frankses were experts on sea lions and caves. Why wouldn't they buy their own copy? Mr. C. said they're rich." Alex tucked her legs beneath her.

McKenzie folded her arms behind her head and sighed. "I don't know why anyone would steal the book and leave Mr. C.'s valuables, but I'll do everything I can to find out!"

CHAPTER 7

A Cruel Hoax

"The tour doesn't start for twenty minutes," Alex said while the girls waited outside the Sea Lion Harbor lobby the next morning. "Why don't you stand by the sign, and I'll tape you. When I tell you to begin, start saying what we rehearsed."

McKenzie stood by the sign, trying to act like a professional news reporter. When Alex motioned for her to begin, she smiled at the camera and spoke. "Hi, I'm McKenzie Phillips, and I'm standing outside the Sea Lion Harbor observation area on the gorgeous Oregon coast. In just a few minutes, we'll go inside the cave and take a close-up look at the amazing Steller sea lions.

"The Steller sea lion is in the same family as the seal," McKenzie continued. "But the sea lion has an external ear flap while a seal only has a tiny opening for an ear. To move through the water, sea lions move their front flippers up and down. They walk on all four flippers on the ground, while seals scoot around. Let's go inside and take a look at the fascinating Sea Lion Harbor."

"Great!" Alex said, lowering the recorder. "I'll record more after we get inside."

A steady stream of people of all ages hurried past them, forming lines at the ticket booth. Others stopped to pose in front of the large brass sea lion statue out front and have their picture taken.

"Let's go." Alex grabbed McKenzie's arm. "People are lining up for tickets already."

After paying their admission, the girls stepped inside the lobby and waited for the tour to begin. A young man wearing a red polo shirt and matching cap approached their group of about fifteen people. He had long blond hair and looked about twenty years old.

"Hi. I'm Colby, your tour guide. If you've never been to Sea Lion Harbor before, you're in for a treat. I see most of you dressed warmly. That's good. It gets chilly down in the cave. Let's get started. Follow me, folks."

The girls hurried down the hall following Colby as he led the group down a set of stairs to an elevator.

"Once the elevator lowers us two hundred feet down, we'll take more stairs and climb farther down to the observation area," Colby explained as the elevator descended. "A few sea lions may be inside the cave, but most of them will be outside on the rocky ledges. In the spring and summer, sea lions prefer to be outside in the fresh air."

McKenzie felt her stomach twitch as the elevator dropped lower and lower into the ground. After they reached the bottom, they stepped out of the elevator. The girls followed Colby and the rest of the group down a set of stairs. Tiny lights set into the wall lit their way.

McKenzie peered over the railing into the darkness of the cave. The air smelled damp and musty. McKenzie shivered despite the sweatshirt she had worn. Alex was at the end of the line, recording every minute with her video recorder.

At the bottom of the stairs, they turned a corner and stepped into a well-lit observation area. Water from the cove rushed through a tunnel, forming a natural pool at the bottom of the cave. Though only a few sea lions gathered in the pool, they sounded like a thousand. Their barking echoed off the cave walls.

McKenzie searched the group of sea lions, hoping to see Mario and Bianca. She was praying that the two pups had somehow gotten separated from their mother, Susie, and made their way in here. She knew it was not likely, but she couldn't help hoping. Scanning the herd of sea lions, she groaned inwardly.

They're not here, either, she thought dismally.

Down inside, McKenzie felt guilty for suspecting the Frankses of stealing the pups. Though the young boy claimed he had seen the theft, he could have been mistaken. But the description of the man's fish tattoo seemed too coincidental. McKenzie felt the boy was speaking the truth. *But why would anyone steal some of God's precious animals? If the Frankses actually stole them, surely they knew it was illegal,* McKenzie thought.

"Let's record some more here," Alex said as she tugged McKenzie into position in front of the railing.

"I can't hear a thing you're saying!" McKenzie yelled over the din of the barking sea lions behind them.

"This could be interesting!" Alex practically screamed in McKenzie's ear. "But let's try it."

After several attempts at recording McKenzie's report, Alex broke into a fit of giggles. "All I can see through the viewfinder is your mouth moving, while the sea lions are barking their heads off. It almost looks like you're barking your head off, too!"

"Maybe I can report separately, when we get away from all this noise," McKenzie said.

The girls hurried to catch up with Colby and the rest of the group who had left the observation area. The tour guide led the group outside, down another set of stairs to the outdoor viewpoint. As Alex recorded the herd of sea lions on the rocky ledge, McKenzie stepped closer to the tour group.

"Can sea lions be hunted?" a man asked.

"No, it is illegal to hunt sea lions," Colby answered. "The number of Steller sea lions have decreased over the years. But since laws are in place to protect all marine mammals, hopefully their numbers will increase."

McKenzie pulled a notebook from her backpack and scribbled notes in case she needed them later. As she turned to head back to Alex, Colby's voice caught her attention.

"Many people love to watch the sea lions at play. They adapt well to captivity and are natural entertainers." Colby pointed out several sea lions putting on a show for the audience by spinning in the water.

The group gathered at the railing, watching the sea lions frolic below them. Alex paced about the upper ledge, recording the animals from various angles.

McKenzie's mind was lost in thought when she felt her cell phone vibrate in her pocket. Stepping away from the barking sea lions, she saw Bailey's phone number on the screen.

"Hey, Bailey," McKenzie answered, plugging her other ear with her finger to drown out the background noise.

"I can hardly hear you," Bailey said. "What's all that noise?"

"We're at the Sea Lion Harbor taking a tour. That barking is from the sea lions," McKenzie explained.

"Well, I just wanted to tell you I've been researching sea lions. I found an Internet article that says they make great performers in circus acts and marine shows," Bailey said.

"Really? That's cool," McKenzie said. "I wonder what kinds of acts they can do."

"I don't know," Bailey said. "The article didn't say. Maybe the thieves want to sell them for an act, though."

McKenzie thought for a moment. "That's an idea, anyway. Maybe I can ask our tour guide about it."

After saying good-bye to Bailey, McKenzie hung up and stuffed the phone in her pocket. The group had scattered about the observation area, many of them snapping pictures.

While she waited for Alex to finish taping the sea lions, McKenzie walked over to Colby. He was leaning on an iron railing, staring at the sea lions below. He looked up as she approached.

"My friend and I are doing a video report for a public TV station. Could I ask you a few questions?" McKenzie asked.

"Shoot," Colby answered, still leaning on the railing.

"We're trying to figure out what happened to the missing sea lion pups." McKenzie held her notepad and pen, poised to write. "A friend of mine said that sea lions are used for circus acts. Is that true?"

Colby's eyes narrowed. "Yes, some shows around the country use them for entertainment."

"How and where are sea lions trained?" McKenzie continued.

Colby stood up straight, looking at her with piercing eyes. He paused and asked, "What do you know about these missing pups?"

"Nothing, really," McKenzie said, wondering why he didn't answer her question. "We heard they might have been stolen, so we're trying to figure out where the thieves might have taken them."

"So, you think you can find these baby sea lions?" Colby smirked.

"Well, we're pretty good at solving mysteries," McKenzie explained. "We have some clues already."

Colby's eyes narrowed as he folded his arms across his chest. "What kind of clues?"

McKenzie suddenly felt uncomfortable. *Why is he so concerned about the information we have?* she wondered while Colby tapped his foot.

"Well, we have a description of the couple seen taking them. Since sea lions are used in circus acts, I'm wondering if the thieves are planning to train and sell them. If we could get inside a training center, maybe we could find the pups," McKenzie said.

Colby turned away and stared absentmindedly at the sea lions in the cove.

Did I say something wrong? McKenzie wondered. *He acts almost upset with me for asking about Mario and Bianca.*

After a minute, Colby turned back to McKenzie. "I know somebody who may have answers for you. Let me make a quick phone call."

McKenzie took a deep breath. *He must not be mad after all if he wants to help. Maybe he's just concerned about the sea lions.*

Colby walked to the far side of the observation area. He pulled a cell phone from a clip at his waist. He glanced at McKenzie, then turned his back to her. The noise of the sea lions was so loud that she couldn't hear a word he said on the phone.

A movement behind McKenzie caught her attention. Turning, she saw Alex approaching. McKenzie quickly filled her in on her phone call with Bailey and her conversation with Colby.

The girls waited anxiously until Colby returned. "Well, girls, I have a surprise for you. I called Sea Park and told them about your video report and your questions. They are happy to help you out. The moment this tour is over, they want you to come for a special tour of the park. Someone there will have all the answers for you."

McKenzie's jaw dropped open as she looked at Alex, then back at Colby. "Really? We can do that?"

"They're making an exception. Go through the main doors to the souvenir shop and ask for Nina. Don't mention this to anyone else, though. This isn't something they normally do. But since you're doing this special report, they wanted to help out."

"Do we need tickets?" McKenzie asked, glancing at her watch.

"No. Just tell the cashier I sent you. You should have no problem," Colby said with a pleased expression. "Oh, and be sure to bring your video camera. You'll want to take pictures of the marine animals."

"We'll have to ask my Aunt Becca first. She'll be here in a few minutes. But I'm sure it'll be okay," McKenzie said with excitement.

"All right, then. I'll call Sea Park and let them know it's all set," Colby said as he walked over to the railing and motioned for the tour group to gather.

McKenzie and Alex were so excited they barely heard Colby as he wrapped up the tour. "If the Frankses are hiding the sea lion pups there, maybe we'll find them," McKenzie whispered to her friend.

McKenzie called out "thank you" to Colby and

headed to the parking lot as she saw Aunt Becca's car. Both girls began talking at once as they climbed in the backseat. They told her all about the Sea Lion Harbor tour and Colby's offer of a tour at Sea Park.

"I've never heard of them giving free tours," Aunt Becca said skeptically as she turned up the air-conditioning. "That must be something new they've started. I can drop you two off there while I run errands. After that, we're going on the Cape Perpetua tour. You'll love it. The views from the top of the lighthouse are amazing. You can see for miles."

A few minutes later Aunt Becca dropped them off at Sea Park. She promised to come pick them up the minute they called and told her they were finished.

A line was forming outside for the next show, so the girls moved around the crowd. The souvenir shop next to the lobby was busy with people waiting to get tickets. The girls passed row after row of sea lion knickknacks, T-shirts, and stuffed toy sea lions. Slinking through the crowd, the girls walked to the cashier's counter and waited their turn.

"We're looking for Nina," McKenzie said to a black-haired young man with "Warren" on his name tag.

"She stepped out for a while. Can I help you?" he asked as he tucked a receipt into the cash register drawer.

"We're here for a private tour of Sea Park," McKenzie explained.

Warren looked quizzically at the girls. "I've never heard of any private tours."

"Colby, the tour guide at Sea Lion Harbor, arranged it. He set it up," McKenzie stated firmly. "He said to ask for Nina."

Warren reached for the phone. "That figures," he muttered. "Those Frankses are only here in the summer, but they're always pulling stuff like this, acting like they own the place."

The Frankses? Could Colby and Nina be related to Mel and Tia Franks? Oh no! McKenzie thought. *I told Colby we were trying to solve the mystery of the missing sea lion pups.*

McKenzie turned to Alex while she listened to Warren's phone conversation. "Hey, Nina. The kids are here that your brother sent over for a tour. Do you know anything about it?"

Warren listened and then turned his back to them, muttering into the receiver, "What do you mean, you want me to give the tour? Okay, okay. I'll show them the tanks."

Warren groaned as he hung up the phone. He motioned for the girls to follow him. "Come on. Let's go."

He told his assistant he was leaving and ushered

the girls out a side door past the crowd of people lined up for the show. He led them down a long concrete hallway lined with several metal doors. A damp, fishy smell wafted up the empty corridor. The girls' footsteps echoed as their shoes slapped the cement floor.

Something is really strange, McKenzie thought. *No one seems to know anything about this tour.*

McKenzie swallowed and spoke to Warren, "I'm really sorry, but Colby set it all up. We're doing a video report for public TV, and we go home in a few days."

Warren turned and gave a slight smile. "It's not your fault. Colby and Nina think just because their parents are trainers that they can do anything they want. Actually, I need a break from the souvenir shop anyway."

"So Colby and Nina are Mel and Tia Franks' kids?" McKenzie asked.

"Yep," he said, stopping at a door with a tiny glass window in it. "They sure are. Nina wanted to make sure I showed you the inside of this room. In here you'll see the tank where we train some of our sea mammals."

Warren opened the door. Alex lifted her camcorder and swept the viewfinder across the room. A large tank sat in the center of the room, with ledges built along the sides. At first McKenzie thought the tank was empty, but then she saw dark shadows near the far end.

She stared at the two shimmering gray bodies beneath the water. Her jaw dropped open, and her heart pumped wildly. The two mammals swimming in the tank looked exactly like Mario and Bianca!

CHAPTER 8

Suspicions!

McKenzie edged toward the tank for a closer look. The two mammals swam forward and raised their heads out of the water. McKenzie's heart sank. They weren't Mario and Bianca, after all. They weren't even sea lions; they were young seals.

"For a minute, I thought we'd found the missing sea lion pups," McKenzie said with disappointment.

"Yes, from a distance, seals look a little like sea lions." Alex stepped forward and stopped recording.

Warren grabbed a beach ball from a basket on the floor and tossed it into the tank. "Everyone seems concerned about Mario and Bianca. But you won't find them here, that's for sure. We get all of our mammals through reputable sources. Supposedly some kid saw the sea lion pups being stolen. If that's the case, the thief will probably sell them on the black market."

"Where?" Alex asked as she watched the seals playing.

"'Black market' means selling something illegally,"

Warren explained as he walked to the far side of the tank and leaned on the edge.

McKenzie thought about that for a moment. "Why would anyone want to steal a sea lion and sell it?"

Warren shrugged his shoulders and glanced at his watch. "It's hard to tell. Maybe some kind of collection. Twin sea lions are rare."

"What happens to the animals that are trained here?" McKenzie asked, watching the seals swim toward the beach ball.

"We only train animals we're going to use in our shows," Warren said. "We're planning to add these two seals to our main attraction."

"Are your trainers working with any sea lions right now?" McKenzie asked hopefully.

"No. We're concentrating on these two seals," Warren said. "Training is a lot of hard work."

McKenzie frowned. She watched Alex film the seals playing with the ball. *This isn't what I was hoping to find out. I really thought I would find Mario and Bianca in here. But all they have are seals,* she thought with dismay. *Maybe the Frankses aren't the thieves, after all.*

The seals flung their upper bodies from the water and popped the ball into the air. When it plopped back into the tank, they scooted it around and around. One seal came up beneath it and flung it in an arch toward the girls. McKenzie reached out her arms and caught it, showering Alex with a spray of water.

"Toss it back in," Warren said with a laugh.

The girls watched in amazement as the seals played with the ball. They were so absorbed in the show that they didn't notice anyone had arrived. Then a man called out. "Okay, Warren, I'll take over now."

McKenzie turned. Mel Franks stood in the doorway. Beside him stood a young woman with straight brown hair, wearing a khaki-colored fishing cap pulled low over her forehead. She disappeared through a door that looked like it led into a storeroom.

She looks familiar. McKenzie's stomach began to churn.

"Hey, Mr. Franks, I didn't know you were here," Warren said with surprise. "I'm giving these girls a behind-the-scenes tour. They said Colby arranged it. Do you know anything about it?"

"Of course," Mr. Franks said, smiling at the girls. "I'm glad we could accommodate you so quickly. Do you have any questions? We need to get busy with our training in here."

"I thought training was over for the day," Warren said with a confused look.

"These seals need more work," Mr. Franks said with

an annoyed tone. "Why don't you head back to the lobby, Warren? We'll take over from here."

"Well, sure," Warren said, surprised. "I'll leave the girls to you then. We were just starting the tour. This was our first stop."

The girls thanked Warren and watched him head out the door. McKenzie suddenly had a funny feeling. *Was that girl his daughter, Nina?* she wondered. *She does kind of look like Mrs. Franks.*

Mr. Franks ignored the girls. He reached into the tank and retrieved the ball. He tossed it into the large basket against the wall.

"Did Warren answer all your questions?" Mr. Franks asked, turning to the girls.

McKenzie thought for a moment, then spoke. "I thought for sure we had found the missing sea lion pups when we first came in here. These seals look so much like them."

Mr. Franks' tone of voice softened. "Seals and sea lions can easily be confused. Like I told you the other day, killer whales probably got the pups. You should probably give up on ever seeing them again. It's just one of those things."

I think he's trying to convince us that the pups are dead, McKenzie thought. *Does he have something to hide?*

"Are you guys the only trainers at Sea Park?" McKenzie asked, forcing herself to look Mr. Franks in the eye.

"Yes, my wife and I train most of the sea mammals, but we're teaching our daughter here to help out," Mr. Franks answered with a stern gaze.

Nina emerged from the storeroom carrying two wet suits. After tossing the suits on top of a black duffel bag, she glanced at her watch. "Don't you think we should start training, Dad? It's getting late."

"Good idea." Mr. Franks kept his gaze fixed on the girls. "I hate to cut your tour short, girls, but we've had a change of plans. We have to do one more training session today, and the seals train better without an audience. Why don't you scoot on out of here?"

Mr. Franks seemed almost anxious to get rid of them. *Is he upset with Colby for arranging this tour without their permission?* Their tour had amounted to viewing seals in a tank, and now they were finished. *This is too weird. Something is going on here, but what?*

She knew she should leave. But she also knew this might be her only chance to ask a few questions about the missing sea lion pups.

Taking a deep breath, she forced herself to get straight to the point. "Do you have a permit to capture sea mammals for your show at Sea Park?"

Nina glared at her and disappeared into the storeroom again.

Mr. Franks walked toward McKenzie, his dark eyes blazing. "What's this all about?"

McKenzie took a step backward. "Some kid said he saw a man with a fish tattoo and a woman take the sea lions. And you have a fish tattoo."

The moment the words came out of her mouth, McKenzie wished she could take them back. *I can't believe I just accused them of stealing!*

Mr. Franks was silent. Then he threw his head back and laughed. "So that's what you two are getting at. You think we stole the sea lion pups?"

McKenzie's face burned with embarrassment as Mr. Franks turned to his daughter, standing just inside the storeroom door. Nina chuckled.

"I admire your spunk, kiddo," Mr. Franks said. "But the kid was mistaken. He saw Tia and me getting these two little seals. And, yes, we have a permit to capture them.

"You might as well forget about Mario and Bianca, or whatever their names are," he said. "I'm sure they're long gone."

McKenzie touched Alex's arm lightly and turned back to the Frankses. "I'm sorry. We just care about Susie's pups, that's all."

"No harm done," Mr. Franks said as he ushered the girls to the door. He still acted cheerful. But a flash of anger remained in his eyes. "Can you find your way out?"

McKenzie assured Mr. Franks they knew the route back to the lobby.

"Let's go," Alex said softly, tugging McKenzie's arm. "We need to get to Cape Perpetua so I can photograph the whales. By the time we get there, it will be time for the tour."

The girls stepped into the hallway and let the heavy door close behind them.

"Oh, Alex! I was awful," McKenzie said, guilt bubbling inside of her. "I accused them without evidence. I feel terrible."

"If it makes you feel any better, I was thinking the same thing," Alex said sympathetically. "We thought because he had a fish tattoo that he was the thief. I can see now that the little boy was mistaken. Seals look a lot like sea lions. He probably didn't know the difference. Don't feel bad. You did the right thing and apologized."

McKenzie nodded but didn't feel any better inside. When they came to a corner, she realized she didn't know which hall they had taken. She looked at Alex. "Do you know how to get out?"

"I was too busy filming to pay attention." Alex looked both ways down the hall.

"I thought I knew," McKenzie said, peering down the hall to her right. "But now I'm not sure."

While they considered their next move, Alex pointed to her left. "I think I hear voices. Let's see if we can find someone to ask."

The girls headed toward the voices and stopped when they came to an open door. An angry voice floated out. "These coolers were full of fish yesterday. Now this one is half empty. And one of our portable coolers is missing, too."

Another voice responded, "You know, I thought there were fish missing a couple of days ago. Our animals can't eat that much. Where's it all going?"

McKenzie peered through the doorway and saw two teenage boys surveying the contents of the coolers on the back wall. At first the boys didn't notice them, but then the taller one turned and glanced at them.

"Do you know how to get out of here?" McKenzie called across the room. "We're sort of lost."

The shorter boy waved a fish in one hand as he spoke, "If you're looking for the front door, you're way off track. You probably don't want to go that way, though. A show is going on and is about to let out. But if you want the back door leading to the employee parking lot, head down the hall to your right and go through the exit door."

After thanking the boys, the girls hurried down the hallway and out the door with Exit lit in red letters. They walked between the parked cars toward a stone wall that separated the lot from the street. Finding a shady spot, the girls hopped onto the wall, while McKenzie called Aunt Becca.

"She'll be here in about ten minutes," McKenzie said, flipping her phone shut.

While they waited, movement at the far end of the lot caught McKenzie's eye. A short-haired blond woman had come from behind the far end of the building carrying a large duffel bag. She climbed into a white pickup parked nearby and backed it up to a door on the side of the building. McKenzie recognized the man who quickly stepped out and loaded a portable cooler into the truck. After throwing a tarp over it, he climbed into the front seat.

Nudging Alex, she said excitedly, "Look. Mr. Franks is leaving. But who was that girl with him? He told us he had to train the seals. That didn't take long."

"Maybe Nina is training them," Alex suggested.

The girls watched the pickup disappear down the street into the busy flow of traffic.

"That woman was too far away to get a good look at her," McKenzie said, frustrated. "But wasn't she dressed like Nina?"

Alex thought for a minute. "I think you're right. Do you think the woman in the pickup was Nina? But her hair was different. Do you think she was wearing a wig earlier?"

"You know, that hat looked like one of those funny disguises we saw in Emerald Bay's gift shop the other day. Maybe she was trying to disguise herself." McKenzie grew excited.

"Why would she do that?" Alex asked.

McKenzie thought for a moment. "The person I saw in Mr. C.'s cabin had short blond hair, and so did the girl we saw in the truck."

"So you think Nina was the person you saw on Mr. C.'s sun porch?" Alex asked.

"It could have been her. When I stepped outside that night to get my camera, I bet she saw me. That's why she was wearing a disguise earlier—so I wouldn't recognize her."

"Wow!" Alex's eyes flashed. "Maybe we're on to something."

"Something is definitely funny about them, whether they know anything about Mario and Bianca or not." McKenzie pulled her legs beneath her on top of her rocky perch. "Do you remember when Nina brought those two wet suits out of the storage room? She threw them on top of a black duffel bag. The girl we saw just now was carrying a black duffel bag."

Alex's eyes grew wide as she suddenly remembered something. "That one guy in that room said fish and a portable cooler were missing. Maybe that was the missing cooler that Mr. Franks carried out. Maybe it was filled with fish."

"Yeah. I just thought of something else. Those seals were tossing beach balls with their noses. Could they be trained to do that already if the Frankses had just captured them a few days ago, like they said they did?"

Alex shifted her position on the rock wall. "Hey, good point. They must be some really talented seals if they can learn that quickly." She hesitated and added, "Do you think that little boy really did see them steal Mario and Bianca after all?"

McKenzie sighed. "It seems possible, but I felt so horrible when I accused them. We don't know that they had fish in the cooler they carried out or that it was even the missing cooler. We still don't have evidence."

"I also think it's weird that Colby arranged this tour that amounted to practically nothing. Something is so strange about this whole thing," Alex said, swinging her legs.

"Yeah, he was so anxious to help us get the answers we needed for our report, but then Mr. Franks acted like he couldn't wait to get rid of us," McKenzie said.

McKenzie's mind whirled. Pieces of the puzzle were beginning to fall into place, but something still wasn't right. *We've missed something, but I don't know what,* she thought.

"I don't get it. Why would Colby plan this tour?" Alex shooed a fly away. "It's almost like he wanted us to see those seals."

That's it! McKenzie's pulse quickened. "You're right, Alex. The Frankses are all working on this together. When I told Colby we were trying to find Mario and Bianca, he called someone at Sea Park—probably his dad. They *did* want us to see the seals—seals that could be mistaken for Mario and Bianca from a distance. He thought if he could convince us they captured seals instead of sea lions, we would no longer suspect them. This whole tour was rigged to throw us off, so we'd give up on the investigation."

Alex stared at McKenzie with bewilderment in her eyes. "So, what now?"

"I bet Mario and Bianca are alive and well. We just have to find out where!"

CHAPTER 9

Terror at Devil's Churn!

"If the man at the cave did steal Mario and Bianca, where would he take them?" Bailey asked.

McKenzie pushed her phone's speaker button and settled into a lawn chair beside Alex.

McKenzie dug her feet into the sand absent-mindedly, eating her last bite of a ham sandwich as she talked. "That's a good question. We know they aren't at Sea Park. Even if they were in a tank we didn't see, some employee there would have seen them. If the Frankses have them, they must be hiding them somewhere else."

"But what would they want the pups for? Sea Park already has lots of marine animals. So why would they steal animals when they can capture them legally?" Alex twisted the cap off a juice bottle and sipped.

McKenzie leaned back in her chair, flicking the sand with her toes. "Maybe they're doing something illegal—like selling them on the black market. You know, like Warren was talking about earlier."

"But how can we prove any of this?" Bailey said, sounding frustrated. "We have no idea where the sea lion pups are or even if they're still alive."

"We'll both be going home in a few days. If we don't find them soon, nobody will. We're the only ones who think they might still be alive," Alex said.

"You know more about sea lions than we do, Alex," McKenzie said. "Where do they live around here besides Sea Lion Harbor?"

Alex thought for a minute and then answered, "There are probably other caves along the coast where they could live. But I don't know how anyone would keep the pups from swimming away. If the Frankses stole the pups, I would think they would steal more. After all, more sea lions, more money. Right?"

"Could be," Bailey said. "If the Cave Man knows all about sea lions, he would know the best place to hide them."

The three girls chatted longer, then hung up. McKenzie glanced up the beach. They had planned to keep an eye on the Frankses. But so far, that hadn't worked out. She hadn't even seen the couple on the beach or out in the cove in their boat. As far as McKenzie could tell, they simply went to work.

"We could go see if their boat is docked. If it's

gone, maybe the Frankses are hunting more sea lions," McKenzie said.

"Or maybe they're just taking a break from work to go out in their boat," Alex said.

McKenzie sighed and leaned her head back. A screen door slammed. Turning, McKenzie saw Mr. Carney coming down his back steps. "Hey, Mr. C.," she called out.

The older man raised his hand in greeting as he strolled across the yard to the girls. "I've been looking all over for that book on caves, and I just can't find it. I must have laid it down somewhere and forgot where I put it. Those maps in it were really interesting. You girls would have fun looking for those old caves. The minute I find it, I'll bring it over."

"Thanks Mr. C.," Alex said. "But we're leaving at the end of the week."

"So soon?" he asked, frowning. "I'll miss you girls. I like being around young 'uns. I don't feel quite so old then."

"We'll miss you, too," McKenzie said. After a moment, she continued, "Do you remember where any of the cave entrances were around here?"

"I didn't have a chance to look at the map before I lost the book," Mr. Carney said, rubbing the back of his neck. "But in the last chapter I read, I learned there are several cave entrances on public land near the Sea Lion Harbor area and Emerald Bay Resorts."

"Is there another copy of the book somewhere? Maybe at the public library?" Alex asked, popping a grape in her mouth.

"No. It has to be special ordered through the bookstores. I guess I'd better get busy looking for it." He scratched his head as he muttered about where he might have left it. Then he headed back to the house.

McKenzie felt sorry for Mr. C.

"Alex, do you think the book was stolen?" she asked.

"Maybe," Alex said. "You mean by the woman in his cabin. But how would she know about the book, and why would she steal it?"

McKenzie heard Mickey bark and Aunt Becca's door slam. She turned around. There was Aunt Becca, coming out of the house. The dog bounded down the steps, his slobbery tongue dangling out of his mouth. Seconds later he put his paws on McKenzie's lap and licked her face.

"Girls," Aunt Becca called, "I just got a call from my boss. The other pilot scheduled to work this afternoon called in with an emergency. So I need to go in right away and take a tour group up in the Skyview."

"What about Cape Perpetua and the Heceta Head Lighthouse?" McKenzie asked.

"I'm sorry I can't drive you two up there like we planned. But I called the resort and got you on the next tour bus. It leaves in half an hour, so if you've finished lunch you can go over to the parking lot and meet the bus. You'll need to go inside to the front desk and pick up your tickets."

McKenzie pushed Mickey off her lap and stood. "Thank you, Aunt Becca, but I'm really sorry you can't go with us."

"Me, too," Aunt Becca said as she let Mickey back in the house. "You'll love the lighthouse. The view from the top is breathtaking."

Within minutes the girls climbed aboard the waiting charter bus. McKenzie slid into a window seat as Alex slipped in beside her. Tourists of all ages filled the seats. An elderly man with powdery white hair ushered his wife into a window seat before sitting beside her.

Across the aisle, a young mother held a baby on her lap. A brown-haired preschool-aged girl wearing a yellow sundress dug around in the diaper bag until she pulled out a small green plastic pouch. As she ripped the top off, McKenzie caught a whiff of grape fruit snacks.

A group of teenagers scurried toward the back of the bus, filling the last seats. Chattering voices filled the bus as the tourists settled in for the ride.

As the bus traveled up the highway, the tour guide, a college-aged girl named Ally, started giving the tourists facts about what they'd see along the road. Soon the bus pulled into a parking lot of a scenic overlook.

"We'll take about thirty minutes here to look around and take pictures. For those of you who want to hike a bit, I'm taking a group down to the beach to see the sights. It's a fairly steep hike, but it's not long, maybe a half mile down and back," Ally said as she stepped off the bus. "Those who don't want to hike can feel free to wait here at the overlook. It's a beautiful photography spot."

McKenzie and Alex headed for a hike with the group of teenagers and Ally. A few middle-aged couples and families brought up the rear. As they hiked down the rocky trail, Ally pointed out vegetation around the beach. McKenzie breathed in the salty smell of the ocean and various wildflowers growing along the trail. After the group hiked about fifty yards, they reached the beach.

"This is gorgeous!" McKenzie exclaimed, peering at the rocky, jagged coastline. The waves crashed against the cliffs, spewing fountains of water high into the air.

Ally gathered the tour group close. She pointed to a large dark opening in the face of the cliff about a hundred yards away. "On your left, you will see one of the most notorious caves in our area. Hundreds of years ago, it was common to see shipwrecks along these rocky shores. According to a legend, a band of thieves scoured the wreckage searching for valuables. They would then fill their boats with these treasures. During high tide, the caves would fill with water. The thieves would then sail their boats into these underground water passages and deposit their valuables, hiding them until they could return."

"So the thieves had to wait for high tide again, before they could sail back into the caves and get their loot?" one of the teenage boys asked.

"No," Ally explained. "These caves were the perfect hideaway. Most of these underground caves have another entrance, usually higher up the cliff. The thieves knew these underground passages like the backs of their hands. They would enter the caves from inland and haul their treasures out."

"Wow! Is that story for real?" Alex asked, snapping a picture with her camera.

"No one knows for sure. It's the stuff legends are made of—stories that get passed down through the generations." Ally held up her hand and called the group together. "We need to head back to the bus now. So watch your step, folks."

The trek back up the trail was harder than going

down. By the time they reached the bus, McKenzie was breathing hard. She slumped into her seat with relief. The bus pulled back onto the highway. McKenzie's mind raced with jumbled thoughts of Ally's story.

Alex leaned over in her seat, her eyes dancing with excitement. "That legend reminds me of the book I've been reading. A man tried to scare all the people out of an old western town because he was storing oil in the mines. He didn't want anyone to find out about his treasure. He wanted it all for himself. Just like the thieves in Ally's story."

McKenzie glanced around to make sure no one was listening. "You know that cave we went in the other day while we were sailing? It was low tide when we were there. Do you think the water would get deep enough to sail a boat in there during high tide?"

Alex looked questioningly at McKenzie. "I don't know. But a boat could definitely get farther into the inlet, anyway."

"I keep thinking about Mr. Franks capsizing us. Do you think he really was trying to scare us away from that inlet so we wouldn't find that cave?" McKenzie said softly. "Maybe there is a clue in there that would help us find Mario and Bianca."

"Oh, no!" Alex's eyes grew wide. "You don't think

he's got, uh, you know. . .skins in there, do you?"

McKenzie shook her head. "No. You were the one who pointed out that no one would steal sea lion pups for their skins. Adult sea lions maybe, but not pups."

"I just started thinking about how sometimes rich people wear exotic furs. Sometimes for trimming on their clothes. Baby sea lion fur would certainly be exotic," Alex pointed out. "Let's hope he's not doing that! But there's no way we can go back to the cave from the cove. Maybe there's another entrance, like in the story Ally told."

"But how in the world could we find it? We might have a chance, if Mr. C. could find his book with the maps." McKenzie sighed.

"If that woman you saw in his cabin stole it, we'll never find another cave entrance." Alex drummed her red painted fingernails on her camera.

"We can't give up. We have to figure out what happened to Mario and Bianca so it doesn't happen to any other sea lion pups. We owe it to Susie to find her babies."

Ally rose from her seat as the bus rolled into another parking lot off the side of the highway. She announced that the tour had arrived at the Heceta Head Lighthouse.

"Maybe I can get some whale shots from the

lighthouse with my zoom lens," Alex said as she climbed off the bus. "I really wanted to enter one in the photography contest in Florence. But my time is running out."

"I would enter something, too, but I'm not a very good photographer. I'll just take pictures to put in my scrapbook when I get home." McKenzie pulled her camera from its case and looked up. "Wow! I've never seen a real lighthouse."

In front of them, perched high on a rocky cliff overlooking the ocean, sat a tall, round white tower with red trim. A matching keeper's house and other buildings sat nearby, while spruce trees loomed on the cliff above the lighthouse. Waves crashed against the rocky shoreline far below.

Several tourists settled onto benches overlooking the ocean, while others headed for the trail that led to the lighthouse. McKenzie and Alex brought up the rear, stopping now and then to take pictures of the coast as well as pelicans and bald eagles flying overhead.

"I see whales!" Alex exclaimed as she focused on two bounding gray spots in the ocean. She groaned as she lowered her camera. "Even with my zoom lens, they're still too far away."

"Hey, we'd better hurry and catch up. Everyone else is already going into the lighthouse." McKenzie tugged

Alex's arm and they raced past the lighthouse keeper's house toward the Heceta Head Lighthouse.

They slipped through the door as the rest of the group began climbing the spiral staircase to the top. McKenzie peered out a narrow window, feeling dizzy as she stared down at the top of the lighthouse keeper's house. Even inside the tower she could hear the crashing of the waves on the rocky shore far below. *I wonder how many secret caves are hidden in those cliffs,* she thought.

After taking pictures at the top, the group headed back down the stairs to the trail leading to the parking lot. When the bus was loaded, the driver headed toward Cape Perpetua for the final tour stop.

After the bus parked, the girls followed the group and the tour guide down the trail to the shore. McKenzie breathed in the tang of the ocean as they approached a black rock ledge. The woman with the two small children pushed the baby in a stroller and held the hand of her young daughter.

Crash! The waves hit the rocks below them, exploding over the sides and sending a towering spray of water high into the air. A fine mist floated on the breeze. Despite the warmth of the day, McKenzie shivered as the cool droplets touched her skin.

"Wow! I see why they call this Devil's Churn,"

McKenzie said as wave after wave struck the rock. The spewing water reminded her of erupting volcanoes she'd seen on TV.

Alex clicked away on her camera, focusing on the spraying water. She snapped shots of the craggy cliffs. On the distant beach, McKenzie saw a group of sea lions gathered on a ledge and heard their barking. She zoomed in with her camera and snapped a picture.

Stepping away from the group, McKenzie wandered down the rock to a tidal pool set back from the shoreline. She noticed a small pool left behind from the high tide. It was filled with sea stars and shells.

McKenzie reached into the cool water and pulled out a shimmering white stone. As she turned the rock over in her hand, she heard a cry from above.

She turned to see a look of horror etched on the face of the woman. The woman screamed again. Her outstretched arm pointed to the Devil's Churn.

McKenzie gasped. A flash of a yellow dress disappeared beneath the surface of the spouting, churning water!

The Hero

McKenzie froze as shrieking voices cut through the roar of the crashing waves.

"Help!" the woman screamed, trying to dash down the steep path with the stroller.

Everything seemed to move in slow motion. Out of the corner of her eye, McKenzie saw someone jump into the water. She gasped as she recognized Alex's thin figure plunging into the water and disappearing beneath the surface.

"Alex!" she screamed. Her knees trembled as she ran toward the Devil's Churn.

Oh, dear God, save them both! McKenzie prayed urgently.

McKenzie's heart raced.

Alex, where are you?

She scanned the dark water. Her stomach twisted like the fury of the Devil's Churn.

Please, please, please, God. Don't let the little girl or

Alex drown. Help them!

Suddenly Alex's dripping form rose from the churning black waters, clutching a small figure. The little girl's tiny arms clung to Alex's throat like a necktie. Her dripping yellow dress was plastered to her tiny body.

"I'm coming!" the mother yelled.

"Somebody grab the little girl!" another voice cried.

All around her, people scurried, frantically trying to help. McKenzie heard an ambulance siren. Someone had called for help. She realized she needed to stay out of the way.

Instinctively, McKenzie raised her camera to her eye. She snapped a picture seconds before a teenage boy jumped into the water. He pulled the little girl from Alex's grip and carried her to safety. A middle-aged man grasped Alex's arm and pulled her out of the swirling water.

The crowd cheered as the mother grabbed the soaked child. An older woman stood a distance away with the stroller. The mother stroked the little girl's wet hair, clinging to her sobbing daughter.

Scampering up the rock, McKenzie threw her arms around Alex's trembling body. "Are you okay?"

Alex nodded and panted. Water ran down her legs. She flung her wet hair out of her eyes and shivered.

"I'm fine," she said through chattering teeth.

A white-haired man slipped his jacket around Alex's trembling shoulders. He guided her to a rock out of the wind so she could sit in the warmth of the sun.

"You were quite the hero, young lady," he said patting her shoulder.

"Are you all right, dear?" his wife asked, settling beside her.

Alex simply nodded as a crowd of people gathered around, fussing over her. She kicked off her tennis shoes. After pouring a stream of water out of them, she set them on the bench beside her. A young man in a blue uniform arrived with a first-aid bag. He raced to the little girl, still huddled in her mother's arms.

Another young man in a blue uniform appeared at Alex's side with a blanket. The bus driver rushed up with a thermos and poured some coffee into a Styrofoam cup. "Take a drink of this. It'll warm you up."

Alex lifted the steaming cup to her mouth. She shuddered as the liquid touched her lips. "Yuck," she cried.

Everyone laughed as Alex handed the cup back to the driver. A man came out of the visitor's center with two T-shirts from the gift shop, and handed them to Alex and the little girl to put on.

"Some people will do anything for a free T-shirt," he said with a grin.

Alex thanked him and slipped into the visitor's center to change. When she returned, she carried a large bag of caramel popcorn and an orange slushy.

"It pays to be a hero—you get all sorts of goodies," she said with a giggle.

Now that the little girl had been pronounced okay, the young mother pushed through the cluster of people and hugged Alex tightly. The little girl shyly clutched her mother's legs. Alex bent over and hugged her.

When Ally announced it was time to leave, everyone climbed onto the bus and found seats. The other passengers smiled at Alex as they walked down the aisle. Several shook her hand.

"You were so brave, Alex," McKenzie said, turning to her friend. "I just stood there and did nothing. You saved that little girl's life."

Alex brushed her damp hair out of her eyes and blushed. "I guess because I've grown up around the water I jumped in automatically."

"Weren't you afraid you might drown?" McKenzie asked, taking a handful of popcorn that Alex offered.

Alex's eyes grew serious. "I didn't have time to think about it. I could only think about that little girl."

McKenzie shuddered at the thought of what might have happened. Gazing at the camera in her lap, she thought, *I sure hope the picture turns out. I want to surprise Alex with it.*

As the bus traveled down the road, McKenzie rested her head against the seat back and stared out the window. She watched the waves crash against the jagged rocky shoreline. Beside her, Alex leaned her head to one side, her eyes closed.

McKenzie's eyelids began to droop. *Beep!* Her eyes popped open as she dug her cell phone out of her pocket.

The message read that one message was stored.

How did that happen? Maybe it rang during the excitement, and I missed it, she thought.

She punched buttons on the phone and listened to Kate's message. "Hey, McKenzie. I've been doing some research and have found out some weird things. I did a background search on Mel and Tia Franks, and printed off tons of articles.

"I wasn't going to be able to look at them until later, but guess what. Biscuit the Wonderdog pulled a page out of the printer and brought it to me. There was a picture of the Frankses and a story about them leading a spelunking expedition about ten years ago. You know, they explore caves and stuff. They even helped that guy write the book of Mr. C.'s that is missing. Give me a call when you can. Bye."

"Who was that?" Alex asked, opening her eyes and yawning.

"Kate." McKenzie snapped her phone shut. She glanced about at all the tourists and then said softly, "Biscuit has done it again. Finding that dog at Discovery Lake Camp is the best thing that ever happened to us—next to all of us meeting each other. I'm so glad Kate kept him. I'll tell you about it when we get home. We're almost back to the resort."

After the bus had parked, the girls said good-bye to the woman and her children. The woman asked Alex her name and where she was staying. Then she hugged her once more.

"Okay, what was the call from Kate all about?" Alex asked as the girls walked to their beach house.

McKenzie relayed the message to Alex and said, "So, now I'm really confused. I thought for sure that strange woman I saw in Mr. C.'s cabin was the Frankses' daughter, Nina. And I'm sure she tucked something under her arm that night. When he told us his book was missing, I was positive she had stolen it. But why would she want it if her parents helped write it? It doesn't make any sense."

"It is weird," Alex said, trudging up the back steps.

"Kate wanted me to call her when I had a chance," McKenzie said as she unlocked the door to the beach house.

"Why don't you do that now? I can't wait to get out

of these wet clothes." Alex headed down the hall. "I'm taking a shower."

McKenzie grabbed her camera and settled in front of the computer while she called Kate. The line was busy, so McKenzie put down the phone to try again in a few minutes.

Mickey trotted over and laid his head on her lap while she downloaded snapshots from the tour. She glanced at each one quickly, stroking Mickey's head with her free hand. When she got to the one of Alex rescuing the little girl, she stopped and examined it.

I'm not the best photographer in the world, but this one is pretty good. At least, I think it's good enough for the contest. She smiled as she unhooked the camera from the computer.

McKenzie glanced at the clock on the wall. She picked up her phone and clicked on Kate's name again.

"I'm so glad you called," Kate said. "I've been thinking about this whole thing. Maybe the Frankses' daughter did steal the book on caves from Mr. C."

"But why would she steal a copy? She must have one of her own. After all, her parents helped write it," McKenzie said.

"I found a summary of the book online. It's supposed to be one of the best ever written on caves along the Oregon coast. I also read that the maps are thorough. Maybe Nina Franks didn't steal the book for herself," Kate explained. "Maybe she doesn't want you to have the maps. Didn't you say you were talking about borrowing the book from Mr. C. the night you discovered someone was listening from the Frankses' back porch?"

McKenzie thought for a moment. Then her pulse began to quicken. "That's right. She and Mr. Franks know we're looking for Mario and Bianca. Do you think they've got the sea lions hidden in a cave somewhere, and they don't want us to find them?"

"That's what I'm wondering," Kate answered. "I've contacted Sydney, Bailey, and Elizabeth. Everybody is searching the Internet trying to find a copy of those maps. So, check your e-mail often. If any of us finds anything, we'll let you know."

McKenzie's mind whirled as she hung up the phone. *Could it really be that simple? Are the Frankses trying to hide the maps from us so we can't find the pups?*

She looked up as Alex walked into the room drying her hair on a towel. McKenzie relayed everything she and Kate had discussed.

"So, what now?" Alex asked, pulling a brush through her damp hair. "We just can't sit and wait for them to find the maps. We could search the Internet, too."

McKenzie drummed her fingers on the desk. "I

agree. We need to actually be out *doing* something. We see the Frankses a lot, so they can't be going too far. We have to come up with a way to watch them and find out where they're going."

"You mean spy on them?" Alex asked.

The back door banged, and the girls turned around. Aunt Becca stepped inside and set a pizza on the counter. McKenzie sniffed the cheese and Canadian bacon wafting across the room.

"How's the celebrity?" Aunt Becca asked, grinning at Alex.

"How did you find out?" Alex asked with a shocked expression.

"The whole resort knows. Everybody is talking about it. They're all saying, 'You should have seen that little girl jump in the water to save that preschooler from drowning.'" Aunt Becca's eyes sparkled.

Alex groaned. "They called me a 'little girl'? That's disgusting. I'm twelve—almost a teenager."

"Hey, I am so proud of you," Aunt Becca said, giving Alex a hug. "That woman was so thankful that she wanted to do something for you. She wants you and McKenzie to take your pick of the tours the resort offers, and she will pay for both of you. You only need to decide what tour you want and pick your tickets up at the resort lobby."

Alex looked at McKenzie, her eyes wide with surprise. "Really? We can go on any tour we want?"

"That's what she said. So, talk it over and decide what you want to do. Then we'll set it up." Aunt Becca placed three paper plates around the table and poured two glasses of milk for the girls.

After saying the blessing, the girls each grabbed a slice of pizza. While eating, Aunt Becca talked about her day at work.

"I even learned a few things today," she said, laying down her fork. "I took an older gentleman, Mr. Tagachi, up today for a Skyview tour. Years ago, before Emerald Bay Resort was built, he ran a fishing boat off the coast here. He told me about an old sea lion harbor just up the beach a little ways. People used to go there and watch the sea lions."

"Yes, we went there the other day," McKenzie said. "Remember? You picked us up."

"No, not that one," Aunt Becca said. "That's the tourist one. This is another one that sea lions hang out at. The fishermen used to refer to it as a sea lion harbor."

"Where is it?" McKenzie asked with her mouth full of pizza.

"Just up the coast a little ways, but the sea lions no longer use it," Aunt Becca said. "When the state blasted dynamite through the rock for a new highway, the ledge the sea lions used for nesting collapsed. That's when the sea lions migrated farther down the beach to the current Sea Lion Harbor."

"What else did this guy tell you?" McKenzie asked as she flicked a piece of cheese at Mickey. He snapped it between his jaws and stared at her, waiting for more.

"All sorts of stuff. He was quite the history buff." Aunt Becca picked up her empty paper plate and stuffed it in the trash. "He knows all about sea lions and their habitats. I'd introduce him to you girls, but he's heading back to his home in Texas in the morning."

Aunt Becca grabbed the leash from the hook by the back door. "Will you girls finish cleaning up? I need a good long walk before dark. I'll take Mickey with me."

The girls agreed. Aunt Becca stepped outside with the dog dancing and yipping about her feet.

McKenzie sighed as she sat in silence with Alex.

"Maybe this guy would know where someone might hide sea lions, but now we can't ask him," she said. She popped a cookie in her mouth and thought for a moment. She pushed her chair back, propping her legs on the corner of the table. Then she glanced at Alex, and their eyes met.

"Are you thinking what I'm thinking?" Alex asked

after downing her last swig of milk.

McKenzie grinned. "I'm thinking we need to use our free tour and go up with Aunt Becca in the Skyview. If we can't talk to that guy, she can at least show us the old sea lion harbor!"

CHAPTER 11

Up, Up, and Away!

"Are you sure you want to take the Skyview for your free trip?" Aunt Becca asked after breakfast the next morning. "I might be able to arrange a free trip if the plane isn't already full and the other tourists agree."

"We know," McKenzie said, "but then we'll have to fly the regular routine. We just want you to fly us along the coast and look for caves. You can do that, can't you?"

"Sure, all flights are paid by the hour. So we can fly anywhere you want to go as long as we're back in one hour. I can take you up later this morning." Aunt Becca glanced at the clock. "But right now I need to run to the grocery store. Anyone want to ride along?"

"Not me," Alex said, sitting at the kitchen table in her pajamas. "I want to take pictures this morning while the light is good. I'm still not sure what picture I'm going to enter in the contest."

"I'll go," McKenzie announced, thinking of the picture she wanted to print as a surprise for Alex.

"Okay," Aunt Becca said as she cleared the table. "When you're dressed, we'll go."

Twenty minutes later, McKenzie entered the supermarket and headed for the customer service department. While Aunt Becca shopped, McKenzie stuck her camera card in the machine and printed off a large picture. She quickly chose a mat frame from the rack and paid the cashier for both items.

When she and Aunt Becca arrived back home, Alex was standing on the dock taking nature pictures. After hiding the framed photo under her bed, McKenzie joined her friend on the beach.

Later that morning, Aunt Becca took the girls to the airport as promised. Within minutes the Skyview took off into the clear morning sky. The plane skimmed the treetops, and Aunt Becca circled above the resort before heading north along the beach.

"Okay, look to your right," Aunt Becca said as she managed the controls. "It's high tide, but you can still see the cave in the side of the cliff that Mr. Tagachi told me about."

McKenzie peered out the window. At first she couldn't see the cave, but then she spotted a dark hole in the rocks. Water from the cove rushed through the entrance, disappearing into darkness.

"Doesn't that look like the cave we found the other

day?" McKenzie asked quietly, so her aunt wouldn't hear. "Right after the Frankses about ran us over."

"Yeah, I think you're right," Alex answered, lifting her camera and snapping a picture.

"So there used to be a ledge there for sea lions?" McKenzie asked. She tried to imagine what the cove might have looked like years ago.

"That's what Mr. Tagachi told me," Aunt Becca answered from the front seat. "When the ledge was destroyed, the sea lions moved farther south."

McKenzie thought for a moment. *If sea lions used to live in the cave, maybe the Frankses could be hiding Mario and Bianca there. We thought maybe there were clues hidden in the cave, but maybe it's the sea lions. That would make sense. The Frankses really were trying to scare us away that day when they tipped our sailboat over.*

McKenzie's mind wandered as she tried to put the pieces of the mystery together. When she and Alex had entered the cave the other day, she had heard no sea lions barking. *Surely we would have heard them echoing in the cave,* she thought. *Unless there's another entrance! That must be it! But where?*

The roar of the plane made it difficult to talk, so McKenzie decided to wait until the plane landed to discuss her ideas with Alex. The hour passed quickly, and soon the Skyview touched down at the airport.

"I have another tour going up shortly," Aunt Becca announced when they climbed out of the plane. "These tourists are from our resort, so you two can catch their shuttle bus back to Emerald Bay. Okay?"

As the girls rode to the resort, McKenzie's cell phone rang, signaling a new text message. "It's from Sydney. She said she sent us an important e-mail message."

McKenzie couldn't wait to get back to the beach house. *What in the world is so important? Could it be something about the maps?* she wondered.

The girls hurried home from the resort, stopping at the mailbox. McKenzie pulled out a thick, brown padded envelope addressed to her.

Ripping it open, she cried, "The video sunglasses are finally here!"

Alex snatched them from her, and they raced inside to the computer. Two messages waited for them—one from Sydney and one from Elizabeth. Eager to see their messages, McKenzie opened Sydney's first.

This took some digging on the Internet, but I finally got it done! Check out the attachment.

The moment McKenzie opened the attachment,

her jaw dropped open. "Look, Alex! She found maps of caves in this area!"

After printing the maps, McKenzie laid them out on the desk. She quickly located the old sea lion harbor. She traced the dark line that represented the underground cave. It curved and then branched off into two different directions. One tunnel appeared to stop at a dead end. The other one ended near the north end of the Emerald Bay Resort.

"There's the other entrance." Alex jabbed her finger at a dark spot on the map. "Isn't that up by the Hideaway?"

McKenzie squinted at the tiny markings on the map. "It sure looks like it. Maybe we can find it."

Now that she had the map, McKenzie started feeling nervous. *What if we go to all this work searching for the cave and Mario and Bianca aren't even there?*

Alex tapped her on the shoulder. "See what Elizabeth has to say."

With a click of the mouse, McKenzie opened Elizabeth's e-mail.

Hey guys. Thought you might need a little encouragement. I really feel you're getting close to solving this thing. Don't give up. Think how

Susie will feel when you find her pups. Proverbs 12:10 says, "A righteous man cares for the needs of his animal, but the kindest acts of the wicked are cruel."

Let me know the minute you find them.

"I don't know about you, Alex, but I really needed to hear that right now. I was starting to think this was too much for us to handle. But now I know we can do it." McKenzie grinned at her friend.

"I agree. We have to try," Alex said, flipping her hair over her shoulder. "We don't have much time left. We leave the day after tomorrow."

McKenzie glanced at the clock. "We need to look for it while the Frankses are gone. Surely they would be at Sea Park now, training the animals. Even if they come home for lunch, that shouldn't be for a while yet. I think we'd better go for it."

"I'm game. Let's go," Alex said, her eyes flashing with excitement.

McKenzie grabbed Alex's backpack by the door. She shoved in two flashlights she found in the kitchen cupboard and the pair of video sunglasses.

Alex raced to their bedroom and returned with sweatshirts.

"Since we know caves can get pretty cold," she said,

shoving them into the backpack with her cell phone. She slung the strap of her camera around her neck. "Just in case I need to take pictures of the evidence."

"Good idea, but we'd better get going." McKenzie scribbled a note to Aunt Becca and left it on the table. Then she folded the cave map and stuck it in her pocket.

Minutes later, they walked down the service road past Mr. Carney's cottage and the lot of spruce trees. A wooden sign reading HIDEAWAY CABIN marked the narrow drive through the trees.

"I hope they're not home," McKenzie said. The girls couldn't see the Frankses' cabin through the forest of evergreen trees until they rounded several curves.

Alex whispered, "This doesn't look like any resort cabin I've ever seen. Look, it has a storage shed. I didn't see it the other night."

"Aunt Becca told me that the three cabins on this end—ours, Mr. C.'s, and the Hideaway—are for renters staying awhile. Maybe that's why this one has a shed. Or maybe it's just an old equipment shed," McKenzie said.

"Their car isn't here," Alex noted.

McKenzie spoke softly as she stepped behind a stand of flowering shrubs. "I hope we don't have to go into their yard to find a trail to the cave. If one of them is home, we could be in big trouble."

Alex tugged on McKenzie's arm. "See that break in

the shrubs on the far side of the yard? Could that be a start to the trail?"

McKenzie peered in the direction Alex pointed. "It could be. Let's stay in the trees and circle around that way. Then if someone is home, they won't be able to see us."

Together the girls walked through the trees. They ducked behind the shrubbery in case someone was watching from the house. Moments later they stepped onto a faint trail leading from the yard of the Hideaway through the trees.

"It looks like somebody has driven back here," Alex said as she snapped a picture.

McKenzie glanced at the double row of tracks leading over a hill and then disappearing from sight. "These are tracks from an ATV."

She peered back toward the cabin. Only a portion of the Hideaway was visible through the trees. If anyone was home, they weren't outside. She didn't see any signs of an ATV at the house.

"If they have an ATV, I guess it could be parked in the shed," she said.

"It's not big enough for a car, but an ATV could fit easily," Alex said. "Let's go before it gets any later."

McKenzie hurried down the trail, deeper into the timber with Alex close behind. The wind whistled through the evergreens. Though McKenzie couldn't see the seagulls, she heard them calling. The track twisted through the trees before dropping into a narrow valley strewn with sand and rocks.

"Hey, look over there!" Alex grabbed McKenzie's arm and pointed to a dark opening in a rocky cliff. "There's the cave!"

McKenzie scurried to the entrance and peered inside. "Someone drove the ATV in here, at least for a little ways. It's a pretty wide tunnel."

Alex slipped her backpack off and pulled the sweatshirts out. After slipping hers on, she retrieved the two flashlights and handed one to McKenzie. She hoisted the backpack onto her shoulders and said, "I have a funny feeling about this. I hope we don't get caught, especially by the Frankses."

"There's no way they'll catch us. Nobody saw us come back here. The Frankses will be at work until later this afternoon," McKenzie said with certainty.

McKenzie took a deep breath and stepped inside the cave entrance. She flicked on her flashlight and swept the beam back and forth. Shadows danced eerily on the rough stone walls as she pointed the beam down the tunnel.

"Are you ready for this?" she asked, her voice trembling and echoing off the cave walls.

Alex edged closer to her friend. "I guess, but I'm only doing this for Mario and Bianca."

"They'd better be here," McKenzie said softly as she crept down the tunnel.

McKenzie shivered beneath her sweatshirt and breathed in the damp, musty smell. When they approached a bend in the tunnel, she turned and looked behind her. The cave opening, now far behind them, was no more than a dot of light. The tire tracks that had led them into the cave continued deep into the tunnel.

"This is *soooo* creepy!" Alex said in a loud whisper, clutching McKenzie's arm.

"Yeah. We had better find the sea lions, or I'll really be mad." McKenzie's teeth began to chatter.

"We'd better not be doing this for nothing." Alex paused, turning on her flash and taking a picture of the tire tracks on the ground.

The girls crept onward. The tunnel turned and sloped downward. *Whoosh!* McKenzie jumped when something fluttered above her head and she felt a quick rush of air on her face.

"What was that?" she cried.

"I think it was a b-b-bat!" Alex stammered, huddling closer to McKenzie.

Don't look up! McKenzie thought, trying to calm

herself. *Then I won't see a gazillion red, beady eyes staring at me.* She scrunched her shoulders and linked arms with Alex, keeping her flashlight focused in front of her.

"I don't like bats. I don't like bats. I don't like bats," she muttered anxiously.

As they rounded a corner in the cave, McKenzie stopped and flashed her light around. The tunnel had opened into a large, high-ceilinged room. *Something sounds different,* she thought. A strange gurgling and splashing sound came from the center of the room.

Stepping forward cautiously, she pointed her flashlight down into a large gaping hole. A rock ledge about ten feet down ran around the edge, surrounding a small underground pool.

McKenzie swept her flashlight beam across the pool and two grayish brown masses lay on the ledge above the pool. She edged closer and peered downward. Her skin felt clammy, and her voice trembled. "Look, Alex. There are two sea lion pups down there!"

"Are they Mario and Bianca?" Alex asked, aiming her light on them, too.

"I'm not sure. It's too dark in here." McKenzie pointed her light at the far end of the pool. "Look over there. There is some kind of a wire gate on that end. An underground stream feeds into this pool, and someone has made a type of cage to trap the sea lions.

"This is a pretty fancy setup," she continued as she swept her light along the floor of the cave surrounding the pool. "Look! There are lights set up all around the pool. There must be a portable generator somewhere."

The girls scanned the room with their lights.

"There it is!" Alex cried, hurrying to a large metal box on wheels. She leaned over and flicked a button on top.

Ka-chunk! McKenzie jumped as the generator powered up with a bang. Spotlights lining the edge of the pool flickered on. Their humming echoed in the vast cave. The two sea lion pups on the ledge lifted sleepy eyes.

McKenzie's heart raced as she stared at the animals. *I would know these two little guys anywhere,* she thought. "Oh, Alex. We've found them. Mario and Bianca are alive!"

Alex raced to McKenzie's side, bubbling with excitement. "I don't believe it! We really found them." She lifted her camera and clicked photos of the sea lions and their surroundings. When she finished, she tucked the camera into her backpack.

McKenzie hurried to the ledge above the sea lions and peered down at them, calling them by name. As if answering her, they slipped one by one into the pool with a splash.

McKenzie jerked her head up as a rumble echoed from somewhere deep in the cave. She felt a vibration beneath her feet.

"Alex!" she cried. "Somebody is coming on the ATV! We've got to get out of here!"

CHAPTER 12

Mission Possible!

Glancing around, McKenzie spied a dark tunnel on the opposite side of the chamber. "In here!"

She darted into the inky darkness with Alex close behind. Scurrying, McKenzie searched for a place to hide.

The roar of the ATV grew louder as it approached the pool chamber. Fleeing deeper into the cave, McKenzie grabbed Alex's arm and pulled her into an alcove. She flattened herself against the wall, relieved by the temporary safety of the darkness. Peering around the corner, she saw headlights of the ATV reflecting off the rock walls.

"Oh, no!" she whispered with disgust. "We left the lights on! They'll know someone's here."

Alex tugged McKenzie's arm. "Get back! We don't want them to see us."

McKenzie shined her light down the tunnel before her, then turned back to Alex. "Let's go. We can't stay here or we'll get caught!"

The girls fled down the dark, sloping floor of the cave. McKenzie stopped when she heard the rumble of the ATV shut off behind them. Muffled voices echoed down the tunnel. She strained to make out the words, but the people were too far away. Boots thumped on the stone floor, growing louder as the intruder approached the tunnel where the girls hid.

"Someone's over here," a woman's voice called. "I see flashlights down this passageway."

A man's voice yelled something while heavy footsteps clamored across the chamber floor.

A shiver ran down McKenzie's spine as she recognized the voices of Mel and Tia Franks.

"We have to find a place to hide," she whispered. "Turn your light off. One light won't be as bright as two."

"Where are we going to go?" Alex whispered fearfully as they hurried deeper into the cave.

"I don't know."

McKenzie stopped. The tunnel branched into two different directions.

The ATV rumble had started again.

It's coming our way! her thoughts screamed as the roar grew louder. *Dear God, help us get out of here*, she prayed.

She quickly scanned one trail and then the other.

A sudden idea came to her. She pulled a piece of gum out of her pocket and tossed it just inside the entrance to the narrower tunnel.

"That way is too narrow for the ATV. Hopefully, they'll see the gum wrapper and go that way on foot. Then we'll have a few extra minutes to get away."

McKenzie darted into the other entrance, pulling Alex by her sweatshirt.

The girls turned a corner and flattened themselves against the cold, clammy wall. Without the light, McKenzie couldn't see Alex but heard her rapid breathing. The roar of the ATV grew louder as it neared the intersecting tunnels.

"Get out and see what that paper is on the ground!" the man's voice boomed over the idling motor.

A moment later, Tia's voice cried out. "It's bubble gum. I bet those two girls—whatever their names are—are sneaking around here! I knew they were up to no good. They must have gone this way."

Mr. Franks grumbled and shut off the ignition. "Grab that spotlight and let's get going!" he yelled, his boots pounding the cave floor.

McKenzie took a deep breath as the Frankses' voices and footsteps grew fainter. Stepping back out into the main tunnel, she turned to Alex. "Come on! We have to move fast. We're taking the ATV and getting out of here."

"Have you ever driven one?" Alex asked fearfully.

"Lots of times. We drive them every day on our farm." McKenzie flicked on her flashlight and ran toward the ATV with Alex in close pursuit.

As McKenzie approached the vehicle, a spotlight blinded her in the eyes. "Stop, right now!" a raging voice commanded.

Shielding her eyes, McKenzie made out the forms of Mel and Tia Franks as they beamed their lights on the girls. McKenzie swallowed the lump in her throat.

A plan quickly formed in her mind. She leaned toward Alex and whispered, "Now's the time to try out Kate's video sunglasses."

Alex nodded. McKenzie stepped away from Alex and moved toward the ATV. The Frankses followed her with their light, leaving Alex in the shadows. Out of the corner of her eye, McKenzie saw her friend slip the backpack off and fumble inside.

"Just what do you think you're doing here?" Mrs. Franks said angrily.

McKenzie cleared her throat, and her voice came out all squeaky. "We were looking for the missing sea lion pups, and we found them. You stole them, didn't you?"

I can't believe I actually accused them! My plan had better work, she thought. Her knees began to tremble.

"Oh, I see you found cute little Mario and Bianca," Mr. Franks said sarcastically. "Well, you'll never be able to prove it. We've got a truck coming any minute now to take them away."

"Where are you taking them? You won't hurt them, will you?" McKenzie stepped toward Alex.

"Of course we won't hurt them." Mrs. Franks laughed crazily as she kept the light focused on McKenzie. "But I think we need to turn you two over to the cops. This cave is private property, and you're trespassing."

"But you stole the sea lion pups. You just admitted it," McKenzie said, watching Alex return the backpack to her shoulder.

"No one will believe you. Like we told you a minute ago, we're taking the sea lions away. We'll have this setup torn down in minutes," Mr. Franks continued.

"You know, girls," Mrs. Franks explained in a sickly sweet voice. "We're very well known around here as sea lion experts. No one will believe you. Don't even try to convince anyone, or you'll be the talk of the town. And not in a good way, if you know what I mean."

Bzzzzz! Bzzzzz! Mr. Franks grabbed the walkie-talkie on his belt and answered. "We'll be there in a sec. Over."

He walked to the ATV and climbed on. "How lucky

can I get? The truck is already here," he said to Mrs. Franks.

Mr. Franks started the ATV, and Mrs. Franks climbed in beside him. He shoved it in reverse and turned it around. As he headed for the glow from the brightly lit pool chamber, Mrs. Franks motioned for them to follow on foot.

"You girls might as well sit tight for a while," she said when they arrived back at the sea lions' makeshift pool. "You're not going anywhere until we're out of here."

McKenzie's mind raced. *We have to find some way to get out of here, but we'll never get by them if we try to go out the way we came in.* She reached into her jeans pocket and felt the cool touch of her cell phone.

As if reading their minds, Mrs. Franks said, "Forget about your cell phones working down here. That's why we have these walkie-talkies." Turning to Alex, she added, "What's with the sunglasses, girlie?"

McKenzie groaned. Alex slipped the glasses back into the backpack. Mrs. Franks walked away, helping her husband move boxes and trunks full of supplies.

Alex leaned over and whispered in McKenzie's ear. "How will we get out of here?"

"I'm working on it," McKenzie said. As she wiped her sweaty palms on her jeans she felt a slight bulge in the pocket. *The cave map!* She had forgotten all about it. Leaning toward Alex, she whispered and nodded toward the passageway they had just traveled, "Let's head back down that tunnel. It's our only chance."

The girls stood and edged back toward the gaping black hole. When they arrived at the entrance, McKenzie flicked on her flashlight and ran. Her tennis shoes pounded the rocky floor while Alex sprinted beside her.

"Hey, get back here!" Mrs. Franks screamed.

"Aah, leave them alone," Mr. Franks answered. "They'll never find their way out. We'll come back for them later."

When the girls reached the fork in the tunnel, McKenzie stopped to catch her breath. She pulled the map out of her pocket. "Let's see if we can find another way out. We'll have to hurry if we want to save Mario and Bianca before the Frankses take them away."

Alex beamed her flashlight at the map. "We must be here." She pointed her finger at a fork in the tunnel just off the main chamber.

"I think you're right. This tunnel will lead to the entrance by the cove. We don't want to go that way, or we'll be stranded." McKenzie traced her finger along another line on the map. "If we take the tunnel on the right, there's another way out. It looks like it comes out about a half mile north of here, just off the main road. I think it's our only chance."

"Let's go. I don't want to be trapped in here," Alex said with a trembling voice. "What if they don't come back for us?"

"It doesn't matter. They don't know we have a map. We'll be out of here in no time," McKenzie said, trying to convince herself.

The girls hurried as fast as they dared down the passageway. The chill had crept into McKenzie's bones. She walked faster, trying to warm up. A horrible thought crept into her mind. *What if the map is wrong?*

She pushed the thought away and kept walking. *How far underground are we?* A new thought rushed in. She had never before been claustrophobic, but the farther they walked, the more the walls seemed to close in on her. *Dear God, get us out of here, please!*

She halted suddenly when they came to another fork in the tunnel. Turning to Alex, she pulled her map out again. "Oh, no. The map only shows one tunnel. Which way do we go?"

Alex squinted, peering at the map. Then she turned and shined her light back and forth between the two tunnels. "The tunnel to the right looks like it curves back quite a bit. The other one goes straight like the one on the map. I think it's the one we want."

McKenzie glanced in both directions. "Okay, let's

go. We can always come back."

McKenzie started down the left passageway, the beam from her flashlight bouncing off the dark, musty walls. The circle of light began to grow smaller and dimmer. "Oh, no, Alex. My batteries are going dead! We should have only been using one flashlight."

"Shut yours off. We'll use mine." Alex moved closer to McKenzie.

With Alex holding the light, the girls crept farther down the tunnel. *Thump-thump! Thump-thump!* McKenzie's heart felt like it could burst out of her chest. Water gurgled somewhere ahead.

"Do you hear that?" she stopped and asked. "Maybe we're coming to an underground stream."

McKenzie stared ahead and didn't see the drop-off until it was too late. Her foot slipped. Her body crashed to the floor, twisting and bouncing as she slid down a wet embankment.

McKenzie screamed.

"McKenzie!" Alex shouted.

Cold air rushed at McKenzie's face. She shot down the slippery slope on her backside. She flailed her arms, feeling like she was on a giant waterslide in complete darkness. A dot of light in the distance grew bigger and bigger.

Bouncing over a bump at the bottom, she sailed

through the air like a rag doll. She splashed into a pool of icy water. She stood in the knee-high water, turning as a scream pierced the silence. A beam of light flew down the hill behind her. Seconds later, Alex landed with a splash at McKenzie's feet.

McKenzie sputtered and caught her breath. A beam of light waved eerily beneath the water. Reaching in, she pulled out Alex's waterproof flashlight.

"Are you okay?" McKenzie pulled her friend to her feet.

"I think so," Alex said in between coughing fits. "But where are we?"

McKenzie saw daylight coming through the opening of the tunnel about thirty yards away. Pulling her cell phone from her pocket, she held it above the water, hoping it wasn't too wet to work. She plodded toward the light as the water grew deeper. When she reached the opening, she stood in waist-high water, staring into the bright sunlight.

"We're at the inlet in the cove, Alex!" she cried.

Seconds later, the girls climbed onto the large boulder outside the cave entrance they had climbed the other day. The warmth of the rock felt good beneath McKenzie's cold, wet body. "See if your phone stayed dry inside the backpack."

McKenzie sighed with relief as she punched in a

number on Alex's phone. After a few seconds a voice answered on the other end. "Mr. C. This is McKenzie. We need you to come get us in your boat, but first, please call the police. I'm losing my signal. We've found Mario and Bianca. . ."

●—●—●

"Look at Susie," Alex said after she snapped a picture. "She's so happy to have her pups back."

Aunt Becca smiled as she stood beside the girls at the Sea Lion Harbor observation area. "If you hadn't found the pups when you did, the Frankses would have gotten away. The police got to the cave as the truck was ready to leave. Though your video sunglasses worked like a charm, the Frankses confessed again to the police. They planned to train the pups and then sell them to a circus, just like you thought."

McKenzie felt a little sorry for the Frankses when she heard they were arrested. But when she saw Susie playing with her pups again, she knew they had done the right thing by calling the police. She thanked God silently. Without His help they never could have saved Mario and Bianca.

"If I hurry, maybe I can enlarge this picture of Susie and her pups at the photo shop for the contest tomorrow," Alex said, "since I never got a shot of the whales."

I think I'll submit the photo of Alex to the contest, too, McKenzie thought.

Later that evening, both girls handed their photos over to the contest chairman inside the community building in Newport. "You can't see mine until tomorrow," McKenzie said with a grin. "It's a surprise."

After breakfast the next morning, Aunt Becca drove the girls to the festival in Newport. McKenzie held the morning paper in her lap. A picture of the two Camp Club Girls graced the front page. VACATIONING GIRLS CRACK SEA LION SMUGGLING RING, the headline read.

"Wow, we're famous," Alex said with a giggle.

"I can't believe the owners of Sea Park invited us to swim with the sea lions today. The owners are bringing some new trainers in," McKenzie said excitedly.

After Aunt Becca parked the car, the three hopped out. Music blared over the loudspeakers as they walked down the crowded sidewalks. McKenzie could detect wonderful smells from popcorn, hot dogs, and nachos to caramel apples and ice cream. Little kids stood in line to get their faces painted.

"Here we are, girls," Aunt Becca said, ushering them into the community building.

A mingling of voices echoed throughout the hall as people walked about, looking at the pictures on display racks. The girls walked through the crowd, peering over shoulders, and looking for their photos.

"There's mine," Alex exclaimed, ducking beneath a man's arm. "I got second place!" Her fingers touched the red ribbon hanging on the side of her picture of Susie and the pups.

"Congratulations!" McKenzie said, "Now, let's look for mine."

Dodging in between spectators, she finally found her picture. A red, white, and blue honorable mention ribbon hung beside it. Alex's eyes grew wide.

Alex grinned. "I didn't even know you took my picture that day."

Aunt Becca stood behind the girls, admiring McKenzie's picture of Alex saving the little girl from drowning in Devil's Churn. No one spoke for a minute, but then Aunt Becca glanced at her watch. "We'd better head back toward Florence. We don't want the staff at Sea Park to wait on us."

On the way to the park, McKenzie suddenly understood the importance of caring for God's creatures. At times she had thought they would never find the pups. But God had strengthened her faith by keeping them safe until they could be rescued.

Later, McKenzie and Alex stood beside the sea lion arena, wearing black wet suits. McKenzie beamed as a national TV news crew focused their cameras on

Alex, reporting on her rescue of the little girl in Devil's Churn.

Minutes later, the crew followed Alex as she approached McKenzie, their cameras still rolling. Aunt Becca stood beside them, holding Alex's camcorder.

"Hello. I'm McKenzie Phillips and this is Alexis Howell, coming to you live from Sea Park in Florence, Oregon. Today we're going to help train sea lions for the park's most famous show. Want to join us?"

McKenzie slid her goggles on and turned to the two sea lions floating in the pool behind her. She climbed onto the ledge and held her breath. With a lunge, she leaped into the air, landing in the pool with an ungraceful cannonball splash!

CAMP CLUB GIRLS

books from BARBOUR PUBLISHING

Book 1:
Mystery at Discovery Lake
ISBN 978-1-60260-267-0

Book 2:
Sydney's DC Discovery
ISBN 978-1-60260-268-7

Book 3:
McKenzie's Montana Mystery
ISBN 978-1-60260-269-4

Book 4:
Alexis and the
Sacramento Surprise
ISBN 978-1-60260-270-0

Book 5:
Kate's Philadelphia Frenzy
ISBN 978-1-60260-271-7

Book 6:
Bailey's Peoria Problem
ISBN 978-1-60260-272-4

Book 7:
Elizabeth's Amarillo Adventure
ISBN 978-1-60260-290-8

Book 8:
Sydney's Outer Banks Blast
ISBN 978-1-60260-291-5

Book 9:
Alexis and the Arizona Escapade
ISBN 978-1-60260-292-2

Book 10:
Kate's Vermont Venture
ISBN 978-1-60260-293-9

AVAILABLE WHEREVER BOOKS ARE SOLD.